ReGeneration

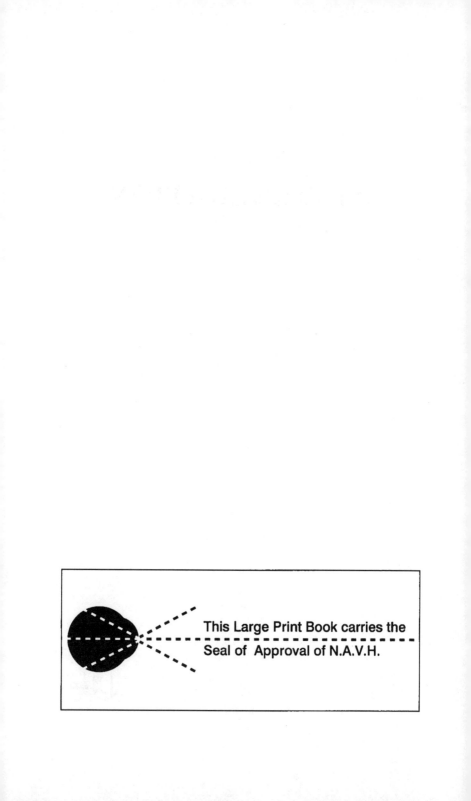

This Large Print Book carries the
Seal of Approval of N.A.V.H.

ReGeneration

L. J. Singleton

Thorndike Press • Waterville, Maine

Copyright © 2000 by Linda Joy Singleton.

Regeneration Series Book 1

Excerpt from *The Search* copyright © 2000 by Linda Joy Singleton.

Published in 2002 by arrangement with The Berkley Publishing Group, a member of Penguin Putnam Inc.

Thorndike Press Large Print Young Adult Series.

The tree indicium is a trademark of Thorndike Press.

The text of this Large Print edition is unabridged.
Other aspects of the book may vary from the original edition.

Set in 16 pt. Plantin.   **3 1969 01279 0324**

Printed in the United States on permanent paper.

Library of Congress Cataloging-in-Publication Data

Singleton, Linda Joy.
    Regeneration / L.J. Singleton.
      p. cm. — (Regeneration series ; bk. 1)
    Reprint. Originally published: New York : Berkley Jam, 2000.
    Summary: The mastermind of an experiment in DNA enhancement decides that the experiment is a failure and that the resulting cloned children should be terminated.
    ISBN 0-7862-3867-4 (lg. print : hc : alk. paper)
    1. Large type books. [1. Cloning — Fiction.   2. Science fiction.   3. Large type books.]   I. Title.   II. Series.
PZ7.S6177 Re 2002
    [Fic]—dc21   2001056328

For a talented writer
and very special friend,
Verla Kay

ACKNOWLEDGMENTS

A BIG thank-you to:

Kate Emburg, for her valuable
plotting advice.
Nina Emburg (Mom!), who loves
listening to my stories.

And

Edwin Emburg (Dad!), my computer and
website expert
http://www.geocities.com/Athens/Acropolis/
4815/

PROLOGUE

The yacht rocked gently as waves cradled it in the dark night. The small boy with ice-white hair shivered, but not from cold. From fear.

"I don't wanna go." He clutched Dr. Hart's soft, warm hand, not understanding why she insisted they leave. The yacht was his home. He wanted to stay.

And yet Dr. Hart, who was so kind, said, "You can't be here tomorrow."

"Why not? It's my birthday."

"Yes. And your termination day. Only I can't let that happen."

Termination?

The boy, whom they called 611B, understood that word. He thought he had learned a lot from listening to the doctors and watching them in the laboratory, and yet there was so much he didn't understand. He remembered the cute white mice he'd petted one day, but then the next day they were gone. Terminated, he'd been told. And he knew it was a bad thing. But how could he be terminated? And why?

9

Dr. Hart was hurrying down the hall and toward the stairs, holding 611B's bag of belongings. "No questions, please. And keep your voice down."

611B quieted, but questions still pounded loudly in his head. Who wanted to terminate him? Surely not Dr. James; brown haired, a soft fuzzy beard, and a good thumb wrestler. And not Dr. Hart. That left only one person: Dr. Victor. Tall and scary, Dr. Victor never joked or thumb wrestled, and never, ever, hugged. He didn't even seem to like 611B or the four babies known as 330G, 1025G, 831G, and 229B.

Now, on the deck, Dr. Hart led 611B to the edge of the yacht, where a small speedboat bobbed on ocean waves. 611B felt angry when he saw the four babies in the boat with Dr. James. Were the whiny babies going away, too? He didn't want to share Dr. Hart and Dr. James. They were like real parents in the books they read to him. Not the babies' parents. His *parents.*

"Come in the boat, Six," Dr. Hart urged with a nervous glance over her shoulder. "I'm afraid I heard something . . ."

"I don't wanna go with them." *He pointed at the babies who slept peacefully in their padded carriers. "I'm staying."*

"No!" Dr. Hart pushed him, so that he tumbled into the waiting arms of Dr. James.

"*Hurry! I did hear some—*"

There was a shout and a sudden flash of fire in the dark. Dr. James dropped 611B in the boat and cried out for Dr. Hart, calling her Jessica. There was another fire burst, a gun 611B guessed, and suddenly Dr. Hart screamed and fell into Dr. James's arms. She looked like a broken toy.

Noises erupted all at once. Dr. James started the boat's motor, an explosion blasted somewhere on the yacht, and more fire burst in the dark.

The babies awoke, crying in the salty wind.

611B hugged himself, staring at the blood on Dr. Hart's chest. Then, like the babies, he began to cry, too.

ONE

I always suspected I was different, but I had no idea how different.

My earliest memories are of blinding white lights and shrill beeping sounds. Uncle Jim explained that I was a sickly preemie and I'd spent much of my infancy in the hospital. And then later, after my parents died tragically in a train accident, I'd taken ill again. More hospital lights and sounds.

Only, when I asked for newspaper clippings about the train accident, my uncle changed the subject. And when I wanted baby pictures for a family tree school assignment, he said there weren't any.

I knew he was hiding something from me.

But on the morning of my first day as a new sophomore at Seymore High, I had something more urgent to worry about. Overnight, like an evil demon, a plump, ugly zit had grown on my chin.

"Oh, no!" When I'd looked at my face, I'd

seen that my jade-green eyes and wide, full lips were overpowered by one huge, hideous zit.

"Uncle Jim!" I yelled, turning away from the mirror and racing from the bathroom.

"What is it, Varina?" My uncle set down his steaming cup of coffee and stroked his trim salt-and-pepper beard. "First day of school jitters?"

"Worse!" I pointed at my chin. "There is no way in the world I can go to school today."

"Why? Are you sick?"

"I certainly look it. Look at my face! It's an outbreak of an incurable disease. I might be contagious."

He peered closely at my face, then flashed a calm smile. "It's merely a blemish. No one will notice it. What would you like for breakfast?"

"A new life!" I groaned and stomped out of the dining room. My uncle just did not understand me. His world was test tubes and college papers. What could he possibly know about an almost sixteen-year-old girl?

Nothing. Simple as that.

With a sigh, I headed back into the bathroom, determined to plaster a whole bottle of makeup on my face. Whatever it took to hide that evil pimple, I would do it. And then maybe, just maybe, I could face my first day at a new high school.

"That snooty Pamela is just *so* not cool," Starr whispered to me as we held our lunch trays and searched for a place to sit in the crowded cafeteria. Strong smells of meat, gravy, and steamed vegetables mingled in the air with the noisy bursts of a few hundred kids crowded under one roof.

I glanced curiously at "snooty" Pamela as we passed a table of kids laughing loudly and oozing attitude. It didn't take a brainiac to guess they were the self-proclaimed "We Rule" crowd. Of course, if they asked for my vote, I'd submit a write-in candidate. Probably Starr. It was pretty cool of her to ask me to sit by her in our algebra class and then invite me to share lunch with her.

I'd always been a loner, the "new kid." Uncle Jim and I moved around a lot, which left me with little time to get to know anyone. I had lots of casual friends, but never one special friend. And so I never quite felt normal.

"Can't believe I used to hang with Pamela," Starr was saying as we sat down at a back table. "So phony. Not at all like you."

"Me?" I held tightly to my carton of milk, wondering what Starr was talking about.

"Darned straight, girlfriend." Starr's laugh was deep and musical. "You don't put on acts. I can tell about people really quick, you know. Like today in algebra, when the teacher was messing my mind with confusing problems, you came over and explained it to me. You didn't try to make me feel dumb by pulling an attitude."

"Well . . ." I made fork tracks in my gravy and gave a hesitant smile. "You aren't dumb. You picked up the equation quickly. And you're smart with people. Everyone seems to like you."

"They do, that's for sure." Another laugh as she tossed back her thick black hair. "Even Pamela. But I'm through with her and those phonies. Hey, there's Raylynn." She stood and waved a chunky blond girl over.

I smiled, thrilled with Starr's attention. It was as if my secret wish had been answered and this new school would be different. Not as lonely. And so far no one seemed to have noticed my zit, so the concealer must have worked.

Seymore High was going to be okay.

Raylynn, sisters named Jill and Janna, and a tall basketball player named Brett joined us. They swapped food (the primo snacks came from Brett's sack lunch) and jokingly dissed other kids, classes, teachers, and even each other. It was a cool experience to be part of a group.

When Starr invited me to listen to CDs at her house after school, I jumped at the chance. Then I added that I'd have to let my uncle know. So when I finished eating, I hurried to a pay phone.

Fortunately, Uncle Jim was staying home today to grade papers. I knew he wouldn't mind my going to a friend's house. He was always telling me to behave more like a normal teenager . . . whatever that was.

So I was surprised when the phone rang and rang and rang before it was finally picked up by the answering machine. "You have reached the Fergus residence, please . . ." I hung up, then tried to decide if I should call Uncle Jim later from Starr's house or dial again now and leave a message.

I idly tapped my tennis shoe on the tiled floor as I made up my mind. I knew Uncle Jim would want me to hang out with a friend. It was such a teenage thing to do. He'd be thrilled. But if I didn't tell him first, he'd worry when I didn't arrive home on time.

So I fished in my jeans pocket for some coins and redialed my house. One ring, two, and then someone picked up.

"Uncle Jim?" I said, startled.

"No," a low male voice said. "Who's this?"

"Varina . . . Who are you?" I tried to remember if my uncle was having any student conferences today. "Where's Uncle Jim?"

"There's no one here by that name," the man stated coolly.

"Oh." Realization hit me and I felt foolish. "I must have dialed the wrong number. I'm sorry. Uh, bye."

I hung up just as the warning bell rang.

No time to try again, so I'd call after school.

The rest of the school day couldn't pass fast enough for me. I kept thinking about Starr and my other new friends, hoping they really were my new friends.

At my last school, when we lived in Oregon, I'd come close to having a best friend — a girl named Shondra who'd transferred late in the term. She'd looked lost trying to find her first class, so I'd shown her around and even helped her open her jammed locker. I had a talent for fixing things like locks, bikes, or VCRs. Unfortunately, I didn't have the same talent for fixing friendships. Shondra and I hung out for about a week, then suddenly she decided to join the drama club. She urged me to join, too, but I could never perform in front of a crowd.

So Shondra dropped me.

Remembering how hurt I'd been, I did now what I always did when emotions bugged me. I shut them off and thought about something new: my birthday surprise.

Next week I'd turn sixteen, and Uncle Jim promised as a gift, he'd tell me a special secret. I'd been going crazy trying to guess what it might be. Had he met a cute lady professor and planned to get married? Had he gotten a huge grant so he would work in a fancy research lab? Or maybe he was going to take me on a vacation. A Caribbean cruise or a trip to Europe, or maybe both. That would be a fantastic birthday present.

While I was enjoying this daydream, my sixth and final class ended.

At last!

I grabbed my backpack and practically flew out of the room, down the hall, around the corner, past the library, and to the bank of lockers where I'd agreed to meet Starr.

And there she was.

"Hey, girlfriend!" she greeted, her frosted mauve lips smiling. She slammed her locker shut. "Wait till I tell you what that witch

Pamela did last period."

"What?"

"Can you believe she told my lame science teacher that she *had* to have me for her lab partner? No one even asked me, and now I'm stuck with that lying pond scum as a partner for a month!"

"I'm sorry. That is so unfair," I said. I didn't even know Pamela, but if Starr hated her, I would, too.

As we made our way out of the school yard, dozens of kids waved and called out to Starr. Some even waved at me, too, so I waved back. And it felt good.

Usually, I felt self-conscious, afraid everyone was staring at me. Did they think I was different? Did they somehow catch a glimpse of the strange tattoo I kept hidden? Or maybe they just figured I was a total zero because I was always alone.

But today I wasn't alone so there was no reason for anyone to stare. So why did I have a prickly being-watched feeling?

Looking around, I saw swarms of kids leaving school; heading for buses, cars, bikes, or just walking. A few kids zoomed on in-line skates or skateboards. Hmmm . . . nothing unusual.

I shrugged and listened while Starr switched her topic to the upcoming student council election, which she planned to run in.

"You'll make a great sophomore president," I assured her.

"You got that right, Varina. The best Seymore High ever had. Not that I'm bragging," she added with a giggle. "Just saying the truth. Hey, I know. You should run, too. Be my vice prez. Wouldn't that be the coolest?"

"Uh . . . I don't think so."

"Why not?"

"I'm . . . not the student council type. I'm kind of shy."

"Why?" Starr's ebony eyes widened in astonishment.

"It's not a choice." I hesitated. "I just am."

"But being shy is a no-win situation. No advantage to it at all. You gotta strut your stuff. Give the world some attitude or you'll miss out on the fun."

"Maybe," I admitted, afraid I was blowing my friendship with Starr already. I could sense a subtle impatience in her, so I added quickly, "Why can't I just help you with your campaign?"

"Sure! You can design my posters. And while you're helping, I'm gonna fix your shy problem."

I couldn't help but laugh. Where had

Starr been all my life? There was no chance of being lonely with her around.

We paused at an intersection, and I took a moment to adjust my backpack. A book (probably my humongous history book) was digging through the cloth, scratching my shoulder. I unzipped my pack and re-arranged the books.

As I glanced up across the street, I noticed a scowling boy; muscular, with striking white-blond hair and a rugged, rough around the edges look. Like someone you didn't want to meet in a dark alley . . . or even on a busy street for that matter. One hand propped up his skateboard and the other shaded his eyes against the bright sun. He looked older, a senior or maybe a dropout, and I wondered if he knew Starr, because he was staring at us.

Change that: He was staring at *me*.

"Starr, let's hurry, okay?" I said, scrambling to my feet and walking quickly.

"Why?"

"Uh, I have to go to the rest room," I lied.

"No prob." She grinned and pointed to a concrete building in the park we were passing. "There's a rest room right there. I'll wait outside for you. Let's go."

Remind me not to lie anymore. I'm no good at it.

With a shrug, I followed Starr.

Walking into the shady, tree-covered park was a welcome relief to the sultry weather. It might be October, but the California skies were still dressed for summer. Unfortunately, I was not. I wore my usual jeans and comfy navy blue sneakers. I wished I could wear cool sandals and shorts like the other girls. But I could never do that.

A few minutes later, I stepped out of the graffiti-covered bathroom stall and looked around for Starr.

She wasn't there.

"Starr?" I called out. "Where are you? Starr?"

No answer.

I called again, and when I heard a noise, I whirled around expecting to find Starr. Instead I found myself face-to-face with the blond skateboarder.

And the expression on his face was *not* friendly.

It was dangerous.

Two

"Where's Starr . . . my friend?" I babbled, backing away.

"Gone. I told her to leave."

"You *what!*" I exploded.

"I said I was your boyfriend from out of town and here to surprise you. That you and I had stuff to talk about."

"That's a lie!"

"Whatever works. Besides, I'm not lying about needing to talk to you. And this isn't something you want your friend to hear." He stepped closer, leaning down so we were eye level, but I pulled back.

Under other circumstances, I might have enjoyed the attention of an older guy. He was tall, with dark brows over intense gray-blue eyes, a strong square chin, and a soft mouth. The blend of dark and light made him interesting, even exciting.

But his clothes were rumpled, his eyes etched with tired redness, and his face framed in dark blond stubble as if he hadn't shaved lately. I sensed something volatile in him; strong angry emotions that simmered deep.

"There's nothing to talk about. Nothing." My voice wavered as I spoke.

"Hear me out."

"I don't even know you."

"Don't be so sure. We met a very long time ago."

"Like I'm dumb enough to fall for a line like that!"

"It's the truth," he said simply.

I glared at him, angry that he'd sent Starr away. I had to find Starr, to explain that this guy was just a jerk causing trouble. But how could I find her? I didn't know her phone number or her address. She'd think I dissed her and would never invite me over again. Thanks to this creep, I may have lost my one chance for a *real* friend.

"I don't know you or want to know you. I'm out of here!" I turned to leave, but he grabbed my wrist in a steel grip.

"You have to listen to me, Varina." His tone had softened, although it still had an anxious, harsh quality.

"You know my name?" My heart pounded. "Who are you?"

"The name's Chase Rinaldi, but that doesn't matter. It's not *who* I am, but *what* I am that's important."

"Let go of me," I said firmly, panic building.

His grip loosened, but his gaze held me firmly. "You have to listen to me. We're in this together."

"In *what?* I have no idea what you're talking about. Are you nuts or something?"

"No. Just determined." He stared into my eyes, as if trying to see inside my soul. And for a moment, I felt something unusual, a connection, like a long forgotten emotion. Way too intense. So I shut out the feeling.

I pulled my arm, trying to break away, but I couldn't. Uncle Jim had warned me to stay away from strangers. And I'd never met a stranger guy than Chase — if that really was his name.

"Let me go or I'll scream," I threatened, trying to sound brave.

"Please, don't." He shook his head, his expression sad, but no longer dangerous. "I'm sorry, Varina. I didn't mean to scare you."

"Now you tell me! Not that I'm scared . . . not exactly. It's just that I need to get home. My . . . my uncle is expecting me. I don't know who you think I am, but you're wrong. You can't possibly know me."

"Yes, I do. I know your deepest secret."

"I don't have any secrets."

"Haven't you always felt different from other kids?"

"Yeah, what teenager doesn't?" I retorted.

"But you're not a normal teenager. You've never fit in with others because of your secret," he went on. "You've always been an outsider, watching and wishing you could be normal. Only you don't know how to be normal."

I pursed my lips together, refusing to talk.

"You *are* different, Varina, and so am I. Your uncle has been lying to you."

"What do you know about Uncle Jim? He would never lie! He's the most honest, wonderful person in the world. You really are nuts! Now let me go or I'm screaming your eardrums out!"

"Think straight and listen to what I'm saying. You're in danger, can't you understand?" he demanded. "Your uncle isn't even your uncle and I don't know what he told you about your past, but it's all a lie."

"You're the liar."

"How can you be sure?"

"Because I trust my uncle and I don't trust you!"

Furious, I jerked on my arm and broke free.

Then, before he could say another horrible word, I whirled around and ran away. I burst out of the park and kept running down the sidewalk, not slowing until I reached the safety of my own street.

Finally I stopped, bending forward with my hands on my knees trying to catch my breath. I straightened, then quickly looked around, afraid that Chase might have followed.

But there was no sign of him.

Relief flooded me, making me almost dizzy.

I was safe.

I hoped I'd seen the last of Chase. What kind of a sicko was he, anyway? And why target me?

I was just lucky to escape. And as soon as I reached home, I'd tell Uncle Jim all about it. He'd know what to do.

Up ahead I could see the red tile roof of my comfortable Spanish-style home and the trim evergreen hedge that bordered the neat grassy front yard. Uncle Jim's gray Ford sedan was parked in the driveway. The car was an older model, but quite reliable. Uncle Jim valued reliability. He said you couldn't always count on people, so it was nice to have a car you could trust.

I wondered if Starr would assume I was one of those people you couldn't count on. Would she believe me when I explained about Chase? But how could I explain when I didn't understand myself? Who was Chase? How could he possibly think he knew me? And why would he tell lies about my uncle?

The whole conversation had been so weird.

Unbelievable.

Shaking my head, I stepped onto my driveway.

That's when I noticed the front door to my house was wide open. Uncle Jim must be in one of his absentminded moods, where he'd spend hours sitting in front of his computer screen, writing articles for science journals or working on one of his projects.

Guess I'll have to make dinner again tonight, I thought with a half smile. *Swedish meatballs sounds good.*

I walked up the front porch and into the house.

Closing the door firmly behind me, I glanced around . . . then gasped.

The living room had been trashed!

Couch pillows had been ripped open, cushions tossed on the floor, drawers pulled out of a cabinet, VCR tapes strewn on the carpet, and papers scattered everywhere.

I couldn't think or move.

I just stared, the horror sinking in.

Someone, or perhaps a group of someones, had invaded my home and torn it apart. But who? Why? And what if they were still here somewhere?

I started to turn, to run for help, when my gaze drifted down the hall. There, in the middle of the floor, I saw a pair of eyeglasses.

Uncle Jim's glasses.

Broken. Smashed.

"Ohmygod!" I cried, my hands covering my mouth. A sick feeling stabbed my chest and I called out, "Uncle Jim! *Uncle Jim!* Where are you?"

From the rear of the house, I heard thudding footsteps and then the clang of the door slamming.

Any fear for myself vanished.

I raced down the hall, calling my uncle's name.

There was no answer.

I opened doors, peered into rooms and saw more damage. My own bedroom had been vandalized; papers thrown everywhere, drawers pulled out, and pillows slashed.

Reaching the last room, my uncle's office, I saw that the door was wide open.

And inside on the floor was my uncle, lying motionless with blood turning his gray hair dark.

Like his glasses, he'd been broken, smashed, and then discarded.

THREE

"Varina . . . Var . . ."

I heard the sirens and vehicles outside, but rather than race to meet them, I stared into my uncle's pale, bloodied face as he tried to speak to me.

"Uncle Jim, don't try to talk now. I called for help and they're going to take care of you," I assured, bending beside him and struggling not to cry. "Everything will be okay."

"No time . . ." He shook his head and slowly uncurled his clenched hand, revealing a torn scrap of paper. "Var . . . Varina . . . take paper . . ." he whispered hoarsely.

"Sure, Uncle Jim. Anything you say. Just save your strength. You're gonna be all right." I took the paper, glanced at what appeared to be names and addresses, then slipped it in my pocket. My uncle's life was more important than a scrap of paper.

"Va . . . Var . . ." My uncle tried to speak, but he was weakening, and I could barely

30

hear his whisper. "Warn . . . them."

"Warn them?" I repeated, puzzled.

His lips moved again, only instead of hearing his words, I heard shouts and heavy footsteps approaching. Paramedics and other uniformed professionals suddenly poured into the room.

Help had arrived.

As I watched skilled rescuers tend to my uncle, my heart pounded with fear and my head whirled with the disturbing question, "Warn *who?*"

Four

I refused to leave Uncle Jim's side, so my first ride in an ambulance was viewed through tear-filled eyes. I still couldn't believe someone had brutally attacked my uncle. Why? Was the attacker looking for money or valuables? But we didn't have money hidden in the house and our most valuable possession was Uncle Jim's computer, which hadn't been taken.

At least my uncle was alive. Just barely. It was unthinkable to realize I might never feel the gentle squeeze of his hand or see his loving smile again. He had to make it.

He just had to!

The ambulance ride seemed to last for hours, rather than minutes. I tried not to stare at the tubes attached to Uncle Jim as I clung to his side, whispering encouragement and love. He hadn't opened his eyes since we left the house, and yet I could feel his need to have me near.

But at the hospital, I was pushed aside.

Doctors wheeled Uncle Jim through restricted doors and into surgery. I was an afterthought, told to sit in a waiting room.

Hours plus an eternity later, I heard a voice asking, "Is there anyone I can call?"

Looking up through tear-weary eyes I saw a rounded white-uniformed woman. A nurse.

"Miss Fergus? Varina?" the nurse said. "Do you have any relatives nearby? Someone who can be with you?"

"Relatives?" This was an unknown concept to me. Uncle Jim had told me there were no relatives. We didn't have the nuisance of prying family. And we liked it that way.

Only right now I wished there was someone to lean on.

"There's no one," I told the nurse.

"Are you positive?" She consulted a clipboard and knitted her brows together. "A grandparent, aunt, or cousin?"

I shook my head. "It's always been just Uncle Jim and me. If there's anyone else, he never told me."

There's a lot he hasn't told me, I realized suddenly. And I thought of Chase, saying my uncle wasn't even my uncle. Absurd . . . and yet it *was* strange to have no relatives. Why hadn't I questioned Uncle Jim about this before? Why had I accepted his simple answers without probing deeper?

"How is my uncle?" I asked, afraid to hear the answer. I clenched my hands together. "Is he . . . Will he make it?"

The nurse glanced at the clipboard again, bit her lip, then shrugged. "It's too soon to say."

"He looked so bad. His head was bleeding . . ." My words were a whisper.

"His condition is serious. That's why you need someone to care for you. A neighbor or someone your uncle works with?"

"I don't know my neighbors. We've only just moved here." I paused. "And the people Uncle Jim works with live near the university, not here in Liberty Hills."

The nurse sighed. "What about your school friends or teachers? There has to be someone you can call. Because if you don't have any friends to stay with, the authorities will step in and place you with a foster family."

"Authorities?" I gulped. "Can't I just stay here and wait for Uncle Jim? I'll be quiet and no problem at all. I promise."

"You can probably stay through the night, but your uncle could be here for days, or weeks. If you don't find an adult to stay with, someone else will do it for you. That's just the way things work."

"But that's not fair."

"It's not my decision, honey. I'd take you home with me if I didn't already have four kids and a house that needs to be bigger." She patted my hand and added softly, "I'll bring you a blanket and pillow. Okay? And if you get hungry, there's a cafeteria on the next floor."

I nodded numbly. Tears sprang to my eyes at her sudden kindness and a lump swelled in my throat. I could sense her concern and felt warmed. Her children were lucky to have her. I wondered what having a mother felt like.

Once I had a pillow and blanket, I curled up on the chair and closed my eyes. I hadn't thought I could sleep, and yet I must have. When I opened my eyes again, there was an eerie hush in the room. People moved outside in the hall, but as silent and swift as night ghosts. I glanced at my watch and saw it was 3 A.M.

I felt stiff and emotionally exhausted. Stretching, I left the room and went into the hall, looking for the kind nurse. I didn't see her, so I stopped at a desk and asked about my uncle.

"He's out of surgery, but in critical condition," I was told.

Not the worst news, but not good, either.

My stomach growled and I realized I was hungry. Food didn't interest me, and yet what else was I going to do?

Digging into my pocket, I pulled out some crumpled bills. Fourteen dollars. It wouldn't last long, but for now it was enough. I found some vending machines and bought a Pepsi, cheese and crackers, and some M&M's. Not a well-rounded meal, but to my growling stomach, it was a feast.

"I like the blue M&M's."

Startled, I looked up and into a pair of gray-blue eyes.

Chase.

"You again!" I cried, distrustful. "What are you doing here?"

He sat beside me in a white plastic chair. "I'm so sorry."

"Why?" I pulled back with fear. "Did you have something to do with Uncle Jim's attack? Was it you? Did you hurt him?"

"Of course not! When I saw the ambulance, I felt terrible. I wanted to help, but I was too late." He gave a deep sigh and added softly, "You probably won't believe me, but I care about your uncle, too."

"Why? What do you know about Uncle Jim?" I asked suspiciously, closing my hand tightly around the M&M's.

"A lot." Chase lowered his voice, although it wasn't necessary because we were the only people in the waiting room. "I know who he really is."

"Please," I said wearily. "No more lies."

"I'm trying to help. Your uncle has already been hurt, you could be next."

"That's ridiculous. I don't have any enemies."

"Yes, you do. We both do."

"Yeah, right," I said skeptically, rubbing my aching head. "How can I have any enemies? I don't even have time to make friends let alone enemies."

"It's hard to explain," Chase said, clasping his rough, calloused hands around his knee, his voice harsh with sorrow. "A lot has happened. Only a week ago I had a normal life — but not anymore."

I couldn't help but be intrigued.

"What happened?"

His dark expression grew even darker. "People I cared about were . . . killed. And it's not over, because the killer is still out there, looking for me, to finish the job."

"What?" I cried. "Somebody wants you dead?"

He nodded. "A man from my past . . . *our* past . . . set a fire to kill me . . . only things went wrong. I overheard him talking to an accomplice on a cell phone. I have really good hearing, and I heard quite a lot. Too much, maybe. And yet not enough to save —" He choked on his words, his face pale and grief-stricken.

I could feel Chase's anguish, and despite my logical doubts, I knew in my heart that he was being sincere.

"Because of what I'd overheard, I knew where he, Mansfield Victor, was headed." Chase's dark brow knitted into an angry line of fury, and he clenched his hands into fists. "So I left. And I'm going to get him, no matter what."

"Why not go to the police?"

"Too risky." He scowled. "Besides, I had to find you and the others."

"Others?"

"Way too complicated. You'll just accuse me of being a liar again. It's more urgent to get you into hiding. You don't really think your uncle's attack was coincidental?"

"Of course not. Some lowlifes tried to rob my house, but I guess Uncle Jim surprised them and got hurt."

"Get real, Varina. Your house was searched, not robbed. And you're in danger."

"But *why?*" I demanded. "There's nothing valuable in my house and there's no reason for anyone to harm me. You're not making any sense."

"You already think I'm crazy, and if I tell you the truth, you'll really freak out. But you have to *know* you're different. What did your uncle tell you about your parents?"

"They died in a train wreck when I was a baby."

"Convenient," he scoffed. "Do you have pictures of them?"

"Of course. Their wedding album, some videotapes, and a bunch of Mom's albums of her childhood."

"What about *your* childhood? Any pictures?" he asked with an odd gleam in his gray-blue eyes.

"Sure. Uncle Jim loves to take pictures, especially at holidays and birthdays." I thought of my birthday . . . next week . . . and my throat tightened. A birthday without Uncle Jim would be no celebration. He just had to get better.

"But what about baby pictures?" Chase persisted. "Like when you were born?"

"They're aren't any. Those albums were destroyed in the train wreck with my parents' luggage."

"A lie. Do you believe everything your uncle tells you?"

"Yes," I said defiantly, although it wasn't

the whole truth. I'd always known my uncle had secrets. But they were his business, not mine. Besides, I was getting tired and irritated with this conversation. What was Chase trying to prove anyway?

"Varina, don't you see? No baby pictures and your parents conveniently died in a train wreck. And I bet there aren't any relatives to tell you about your past, either."

"So?" I folded my arms across my chest, challenging him. "What are you getting at?"

"You haven't changed much," he said with a wry grin. "Still a brat. At least you don't pull my hair anymore."

"Pull your hair?" I repeated in astonishment. "You totally have me mixed up with someone else. Until today, I'd never seen you before."

"You were just a baby." He raked his fingers through his blond hair and gave me a deep look. "I don't remember everything about that time either. It was so long —"

The waiting room door burst open, cutting off Chase.

"Varina?" It was the kind nurse I'd spoken to earlier.

"Yes?"

She flashed a warm smile. "There's someone who wants to see you."

"Uncle Jim?" I asked eagerly, jumping up.

"Is he okay? Can I see him?"

"I wasn't talking about your uncle. There's someone else to see you. I'm so relieved. Now I won't worry so much about you." Her smile widened and she added excitedly, "Come with me and I'll take you to her."

"Her?" I echoed, exchanging a puzzled look with Chase.

"Yes." The nurse took my hand. "Your aunt Ginny. She's come to take you home."

FIVE

Aunt Ginny.

My aunt.

These words echoed strangely in my head, like a foreign language I couldn't begin to comprehend. I wasn't sure what to think or feel, so I simply stood up, glanced uncertainly at Chase, then left the room, following Nurse Burns down a long, echoing hallway.

I didn't say anything as we walked to the lobby. Our soft-soled shoes made airy swooshing sounds. Other hospital noises breezed on climate-controlled air, swirling around me and yet not touching me. I was too drawn into my own thoughts.

How could I have an aunt that I knew nothing about? It was all just too strange. Maybe it was a huge mix-up, some other girl's aunt Ginny. Yeah, that made more sense. I had no relatives. Although when I was little, I longed for more family. Cousins, grandparents, a brother or a sister; other faces resembling mine, similar voices that blended together like a well-rehearsed song, and shared traits and history that created a living family quilt.

"Here she is," Nurse Burns said cheerfully, presenting me to a petite, dark-haired woman with a long, straight nose, a dainty mouth, and curved elegant cheekbones. She wore a white linen suit, matching pumps, and several rings sparkled from her slender fingers. Although shorter than I, she held herself with the grace of a dancer and a proud lift of her chin. Not someone you could forget . . . which added to my confusion.

"There must be a mistake —" I started to say.

"Varina! My dear child!" The woman smiled warmly and held out her French-tipped manicured hand to me.

I ignored the outstretched hand and stared at her face. I searched for recognition, and found none. "I don't know you," I said flatly.

Nurse Burns frowned. "You don't? But I thought . . ."

"Oh, dear." The dark-haired woman sighed and let her hand drop to her side. "I had hoped you would recognize me or at least know my name. It's been a very long time since I last saw you, Varina. You were the most adorable baby in the world."

"I was?"

"A wonderful, bright, beautiful child. And your parents were so proud of you. I was devastated when they died." She reached up to touch one of her dangling diamond and pearl earrings as her expression saddened. "I still miss my brother terribly."

"Your brother?"

"He was your father," she stated.

I simply stared, my mouth falling open and my mind spinning as I tried to fit puzzle pieces together. I remembered the picture of my parents, and my father did have dark hair like this woman, but he'd been very tall, with a football player's husky shoulders.

"How did you find out about Uncle Jim's accident?" I asked.

"A friend of mine who works at the hospital recognized Jim's name, and called me. Of course, I came as quickly as possible."

"But why haven't I heard of you? Why haven't you called or visited? I mean, Uncle Jim never even said . . ."

"Unfortunately Jim and I have never been on the best of terms. Call it idealistic differences, I suppose."

I had no idea what she meant by that, which only added to my confusion. And yet under my confusion was hope . . . longing.

"Varina, we have so much to catch up on," she said sincerely. "I wish we could have met under better circumstances, but I didn't know where you were until I heard about Jim's accident."

"It wasn't an accident. He was attacked."

"So much violence these days," Nurse Burns murmured with a furrow of her brow. Then she gave me an encouraging smile. "I hate to leave you, Varina, but I have duties to attend to. Now that you have family here, I know you'll be fine."

I wasn't so sure, but I nodded to reassure her.

"Varina will be well cared for," my aunt said in a gentle, forceful manner. She reminded me of a dove; small, quick, and swift with purpose.

Nurse Burns gave me a soft hug, bringing tears to my eyes, then she turned and left — leaving me alone with Aunt Ginny.

I clasped my hands together, held tight to myself, and regarded my aunt cautiously. "So now what?"

"That's up to you, Varina. I'd like to help you through this. The nurse has told me that Jim's condition is quite serious. If he recovers, he'll be here a few weeks, or maybe longer. And while I am sorry for Jim, I'm more concerned about you."

I brushed a tear away, feeling a painful ache that went deeper than bone. Never knowing my parents, except through a wedding video and well-thumbed photo albums, and now having to face the grim possibility of losing Uncle Jim was overwhelming.

"Uncle Jim will survive," I told her firmly.

"Of course he will. But while he's getting better, you'll need someone to care for you. I hope you'll let me do that."

I shrugged, glancing down at my sneakers and jeans, realizing a new day was beginning and I was still in yesterday's school clothes. School would be starting soon, too, without me.

"Varina." Her voice softened. "When my brother died, I wanted to raise you."

"You did?"

"Oh, yes! I hoped to be your new mother, only Jim stepped in, and I couldn't afford to fight him in court. I was heartbroken and threw myself into work, which meant traveling to other countries. I married, and together, my husband and I built a business that's made us very wealthy."

"You're rich?"

"Shamefully." She laughed, smiling with pride and giving me a wink. "I hope that doesn't bother you."

"No. Money doesn't matter. Only Uncle Jim . . . and he's always given me whatever I've needed. He's everything to me . . ." My voice broke off, and I hoped I wouldn't cry again. It was impossible to erase the image of my uncle's broken, bloody body. Who had done that to him? And why? And what about those wild things Chase had told me? That my uncle wasn't even my uncle? That couldn't be true. No way.

"Varina, I know you're sad, but I'm here for you." She leaned toward me and I smelled a soft fragrance, probably very expensive perfume. "I'd like for us to be friends. What do you say?"

"I-I guess so. This is just so sudden. It'll take some getting used to."

"So we'll take all the time you need. Together." She reached out to squeeze my hand, and this time I didn't pull away.

Aunt Ginny . . . my aunt. I liked the sound of that.

Six

"Tell me about my father," I asked my aunt as we entered her spacious hotel room with thick cream carpets, stark white walls, unusual abstract paintings, and rich mahogany furniture. "Do you have any pictures of him?"

"Not with me."

"I've only seen his wedding pictures, but none when he was young. Do you think I look like him?"

"No," she said, dumping her cream-colored leather purse on the table. "You're the image of your mother. And frankly I didn't know her well. Her family, including your uncle Jim, didn't include us in their social circle. Back then, they were professionals and we were working class."

"Uncle Jim isn't like that."

"Perhaps not now, but he used to be a bit of a snob." She waved her hand and smiled. "Yet no matter. We have something more important to do."

I gave her a quizzical look. "What?"

"Go shopping! Isn't that what all teenage girls love to do?"

"Shopping?" I blinked, weary and numb. "I've never been much like other girls. And right now I just want to sleep for a while, then go back to the hospital."

"In the same clothes you wore yesterday?"

"We can stop by my house and get . . ." I broke off when I remembered how devastated my house looked. I couldn't go back there, not yet.

"Varina, moping around isn't going to help your uncle. Now that I'm here, I'll take care of you. Which means shopping for clothes and toiletries. I doubt you have a toothbrush in your pocket."

"No." I almost smiled, but then I remembered what I did have in my pocket. The paper Uncle Jim had given me. Mentally, I relived that awful moment when I found his crumpled body and heard his pained whisper to "warn them." Warn who? About what? So very strange. And I wondered if I should show Aunt Ginny the paper, ask for her advice.

She had moved over to a dresser and opened the drawers. "You're close to my size. Would you like to borrow something of mine to wear for now?"

"No. Really, I'm fine."

"If you're sure." She gave me a deep look, her eyes an odd color that I couldn't define. A shimmering silver like mercury, swirling and mysterious. I decided not to show her the paper. Not yet, anyway.

Yawning, I told Aunt Ginny that shopping sounded fine, but first I needed some rest. I was so tired, I couldn't think straight. And if I was going to help Uncle Jim, I needed to think clearly.

Aunt Ginny led me to a private bedroom in her suite and told me to rest as long as I wanted. "I'll wait out here for you," she added.

"Thank you," I said, studying her face, which was soft and gentle, like a real mother. I wondered how different my life would have been if she'd raised me. Very different, for sure. But this sort of thinking was lame. I mean, I was happy with Uncle Jim. And all I wanted was for him to get well.

Sighing, I kicked off my sneakers and climbed fully clothed between crisp white sheets.

As I yawned, my eyes shutting tight, I remembered Aunt Ginny saying I was the image of my mother. But my mother had been a brunette with blue eyes and a shapely, large-boned figure. And I was slim, with too-curly auburn hair and green eyes.

I didn't resemble my mother at all.

How could Aunt Ginny have been so wrong?

A beautiful woman, like an angel, smiled down at me, her touch comforting, and her green eyes loving. "Little Princess," she whispered into my ear. "You're so precious and perfect."

My eyes were shut and yet I could see her clearly. Reddish fire in her long, wavy hair that tickled my cheek as she leaned over me.

"Who are you?" I asked, although I knew my mouth didn't move. I must be dreaming, I realized. A wonderful dream that I had no desire to wake from.

"I love you so much," the angel-woman told me.

"But I don't know you . . . or do I?"

A long ago memory stirred and I felt the soft touch of her hands holding me as if I were a baby. I was small and safe in her arms. And she smelled sweet and fresh, like lilacs blending with an ocean breeze. I wanted her to hold me forever.

"I'll always watch over you," she promised me.

"Good." I nodded contentedly, relieved

not to be so alone anymore. "Then I won't be afraid."

"But you must be careful. Not everyone is who they pretend to be." She smiled sadly and added, "Not even me."

"What do you mean?"

"Trust yourself. And take care, Little Princess. When you need me most, I'll try to be here for you."

I felt her worry, her concern, and her love for me. She was as real as the air I breathed and the sun in the sky. Real, and yet far from my own reality.

And suddenly I was sitting up in a bed that wasn't mine, my heart pounding, with an eerie sense of fear but also comfort.

Had it just been a dream? I wondered, digging my fingers into my pillow and then hugging it to my chest. Or was it something more? There was something so familiar about the angel.

Okay, she had told me to be careful and she'd hinted that someone was lying to me. But who?

Chase was a prime suspect; following me after school, acting as if he knew me, and then accusing my uncle of being a liar. Aunt Ginny's sudden appearance was odd, too. How could I even be sure she was my aunt? Uncle Jim would have mentioned her if she was legit. Only why would she pretend to be related to me?

I reached out and turned on a bedside light and thought harder. Chase was either helpful or harmful. Aunt Ginny was either wonderful or deceitful. And my uncle, who might keep secrets but who would never lie to me, had whispered about unknown persons who needed to be warned.

All I had were confused questions.

I needed facts.

And then I remembered the paper Uncle Jim had given me.

Reaching into my jeans pocket, I pinched it between my fingers and carefully drew it out. Maybe this held the answers.

I brought the paper into the light of the lamp, frowning at the jagged bottom edge that had been ripped. I only hoped important information wasn't missing.

Peering closely, I read off the four names and addresses:

#1 Allison Beaumont
    430 Pacific Tower Avenue
    San Francisco, CA

#2 Eric Prince
    Route 3, Box 77
    Marshall, TX

#3 Sandee Yoon
    1300 Mathes Place
    Apt. #339
    Denver, CO

And then I choked back surprise, almost dropped the paper as if it had burned my fingers, when I saw the fourth name:

#4 Chase Rinaldi
    23 Vesta Way
    Reno, Nevada

SEVEN

Chase!

My uncle knew Chase — not only knew him, but wanted me to warn him about something. Obviously the warning was too late, because Chase had already told me about that terrible fire. How horrible. No wonder he was haunted with grief and anger.

But how did I fit into this? Why did Chase seek me out? I was just a high school girl, struggling to avoid ugly pimples and make new friends in a new school. I didn't know anything about killers.

And then another frightening thought struck me . . . had the evil man who'd threatened Chase come after my uncle? I remembered the footsteps I'd heard before I found my uncle, and felt a chill shudder through me. How close had I come to being attacked? Or if I hadn't interrupted, would my house have burned down, too . . . with my uncle inside?

There was a tap on the door. "Varina, are you awake?"

"Uh . . . yeah." Startled, I added quickly, "I just woke up."

"Can I come in?"

"Just a sec!" I called out to my aunt, then I quickly shoved the paper back in my pocket. Allison, Eric, Sandee . . . who were these people and what was their connection with Chase?

Aunt Ginny opened my door and came inside, a gentle smile on her face. "Do you feel better?" she asked, sitting on the edge of my bed.

"I guess so."

"Good. Because I just got off the phone with the police —"

"The police!" I exclaimed.

"Yes." She nodded matter-of-factly. "They've finished examining your house. So you can go back there whenever you want."

I frowned, not sure I could handle going back home.

"Isn't that good news, Varina?"

"I guess." I would rather have heard that my uncle was well and able to return home with us. It was a relief to know my house was mine again, but I knew the cleanup job was going to be another horror.

Aunt Ginny must have read my mind, because she told me she'd already called a cleaning service, one that, amazingly, specialized in crime scenes. They were scheduled to work on my house this afternoon.

"That's really thoughtful. Thanks." I pushed back the covers and stood up. "Can we go to the hospital now? I have to be there when Uncle Jim wakes up."

"I understand how you feel. But when I checked with the hospital a short while ago, he hadn't awakened yet. And no visitors were allowed. So there's no reason to go there."

"I need to be with him," I said firmly.

"Of course you do. And you *will* be with him, soon. But it would be best if we stayed away from your house, too, until the cleaning service takes care of it." She touched the pearl earring, and kept on smiling. "I'd like to spare you the upset of seeing your house so disturbed."

"I've already seen it."

"Still, I've made arrangements for a friend of mine to oversee the cleaning crew and ensure that they do a thorough job."

"A friend?"

She chuckled. "Don't sound so surprised. I may only be visiting the city, but I have many friends, both personal and business, all over the world. This particular friend is a personal one and very trustworthy. By the time you see your home, it'll be just like new. Perhaps better."

I bristled at the way she was taking charge of my life, as if I were a child. And I did not like the idea of more strangers going through my home, my belongings, my life. Yet Aunt Ginny was only trying to help. And I was too weary, too emotionally drained, to object. Besides, a small secret part of me enjoyed being mothered.

"You've been great about everything, but I can't just wait around," I said impatiently, glancing at my watch and seeing that it was past noon already. My school had probably left a phone message checking my absence — if the answering machine still worked.

I thought about Starr — did she wonder where I was? Or was she too busy with other friends to think of me? If only I had her phone number, but there hadn't been time for that. And since today was Friday, I wouldn't be able to see her until after the weekend — assuming Uncle Jim's condition improved and I could return to school on Monday.

I glanced up and realized Aunt Ginny was talking about shopping again. Guess it was a favorite pastime of hers, because she rattled off names of the stores she wanted to take me to: Neiman Marcus, Macy's, and Nordstrom. Way beyond the budget I was accustomed to.

When I objected, she waved her hand, her bright rings sparkling like earthbound stars. "I want to do things for you, Varina. Please don't refuse. We'll have a fun girls' day out, forget our troubles for a while. Besides, isn't your birthday coming up?"

"Why . . . yes." A glow of pleasure warmed me. She really did know me. "In a week, on the twenty-fifth."

"Wonderful! I'm just in time to celebrate with you."

"Uncle Jim was planning a surprise for my birthday," I added sadly. "He never said what it was. Just that my sweet sixteenth should be extra special."

"Sixteen?" The smile vanished from Aunt Ginny's face. "That's impossible. You're mistaken."

"What?"

"You're going to be fifteen."

"That was last year." I shook my head firmly.

She glanced down at her hands, touching her fingers as if mentally counting. Then her frown deepened to puzzlement. "But that

59

can't be . . . I know when you were born."

"So do I. And I think I'm more of an expert on *that* subject." I almost laughed, this conversation was getting so bizarre. "And I assure you, I *am* going to be sixteen."

She opened her mouth as if to argue further, but then she closed it. Tightly. She ran her fingers through her smooth dark hair and glanced away.

When she looked at me again, her poise had returned, as well as her gentle smile. "Of course, you're right. Sixteen. I never was good with numbers."

"Math is my best subject," I said, sharing her smile.

"And sweet sixteen is indeed a special birthday." She held out her hand to me and added enthusiastically, "Come on, Varina. We have some shopping to do."

EIGHT

If my heart weren't so heavy with worry about Uncle Jim, this could have been the best day of my whole life. Aunt Ginny didn't just talk about having money, she loved to spend it. If shopping were an Olympic event, my aunt would be a gold-medal champion.

I just breezed along with her, swept into her appreciation for fine fabrics, jewelry, perfumes, and shoes. When she bought me a complete outfit: name-brand jeans, a designer blouse, funky shoes, and some cool scrunchies and clips for my hair, I really did try to refuse. But I had to admit, I didn't object very hard. Mostly I loved being a pampered almost-birthday girl. And if Aunt Ginny wanted to spoil me, then let me rot in riches . . . at least for this one day.

By the evening, I was exhausted and feeling guilty. How could I let myself have fun with Uncle Jim attached to tubes and clinging onto his life?

"I want to go to the hospital," I told my

aunt firmly, as we left Country Fair Mall.

"Of course, darling. Let's stop by your home first, though, to make sure the cleaners are finished."

"Well . . . okay." I gulped, hoping I could handle returning to the "scene of the crime." I'd just have to deal with it. "Will your friend still be there?"

"I doubt it," she said, glancing at her side mirror, away from me.

I wanted to ask more about this friend. In all of our time together, my aunt had spoken very little about her personal life. I knew she had a husband, but she hadn't mentioned him, so perhaps they were separated or divorced. If not, he'd be my uncle. Another relative.

My heart began to pound and my hands to sweat as we pulled into my driveway, right beside Uncle Jim's gray Ford. The last time I'd been here involved flashing red lights and fear. Tears welled in my eyes, and I hated not being able to control my emotions. *Get a grip, Varina,* I told myself.

So I steeled my emotions as I walked up the entryway and stepped into my house. The breath I hadn't realized I'd been holding escaped with relief. No overturned furniture, slashed cushions, and strewn papers. In fact, my home appeared as peaceful as before the vandalism. Although, I noticed the pillows on the couch were new.

"So this is your home," Aunt Ginny said as she followed me inside. "It's charming, and so cozy."

I think "cozy" meant small. I bet with her taste for wealth she lived in a mansion, something grand enough to welcome royalty, if they were honored with an invitation.

Aunt Ginny was already walking into the kitchen, where she peered into our refrigerator. "Yes, just as I instructed. Some prepared meals and beverages."

"You ordered food?" I asked in astonishment.

"We do have to eat. I'm staying here tonight, and it's my responsibility to care for you."

This was news to me, but I didn't complain. Instead, I stared at the impressive array of boxed meals, a deli tray, two wine bottles, a variety of sodas, juices, and more. I felt uneasy, torn between gratitude and resentment. She was managing my life again. Maybe that's why my uncle never told me about her. He was extremely proud and valued privacy.

"While you put your things away, I'll fix us some drinks," she spoke purposefully. "What would you like?"

"Doesn't matter. Soda or juice is fine."

I turned and headed for my bedroom, becoming nervous at the ordeal of facing my recently trashed room. I didn't know what to expect. Would it still look like my room? A slow turn of the knob, and then a cautious peek inside. My bedroom was clean and organized, better than it had looked in months. Sure, the bedspread was new, I didn't see the blue pottery bowl I'd made in my ceramics class, and only a few of my glued puzzle-pictures still decorated the walls, but otherwise everything else was normal.

When I returned to the kitchen, Aunt Ginny sat at the table, sipping some white wine from a glass. Next to her, my glass of lime soda waited.

There was a lonely little girl inside of me who loved this motherly attention. Buying new clothes, arranging for meals, and now offering me a drink. Would Aunt Ginny end the day by tucking me in bed and telling me a story or singing me a lullaby?

I almost laughed out loud, knowing I was being childish. Instead, I reached for my drink and took a long, refreshing sip.

"Varina, before we go to the hospital, there're a few things we should discuss," Aunt Ginny said.

"You can sleep in Uncle Jim's room if that's what you want to talk about. I'm sorry the house isn't bigger."

"The house is fine. But I've been wondering about the break-in. I have a suspicion it wasn't random. Do you know of any reason someone would attack your uncle?"

"No."

"Did he have any valuables?"

"As you can see, we're not living large," I said with a thin laugh. "Uncle Jim is only a college professor and he was grading papers yesterday. Nothing dangerous. Although, maybe a failing student could have confronted him."

"A student." She tapped her nails on the kitchen table, her mouth pursed thoughtfully. "A possibility, but I wonder if there's a deeper reason for the attack."

"Like what?"

"I know of Jim's interest in genetic research. Could he be working on a secret project?"

I shook my head, although in truth I had no idea what Uncle Jim was working on. He seldom mentioned his research.

Still, Aunt Ginny was right about there being more to the break-in. I thought of Chase's wild story and Uncle Jim's mysterious list. Something very odd was going on — but what?

I considered showing the paper to my aunt. She might know how to get in touch with Allison, Eric, and Sandee. Sipping my drink slowly, I thought this over. I didn't trust giving the list to the police, but my aunt cared about me, so maybe she could help.

"The attack *was* strange," I admitted. "And it does seem like the vandals were looking for something."

"What?" She leaned forward eagerly, her rings catching the ceiling light and shimmering as if they held secrets of their own.

I bit my lip, glancing down at the gleaming ice cubes in my glass, longing to confide in my aunt. She was so confident and efficient, she'd take charge and solve my problems. But did I want to dump this all on her?

It was hard to think clearly, as if my mind was suddenly swimming in peanut butter. Missing sleep last night and then the Olympic shopping spree were taking their toll on me. I yawned, wanting to just sleep for a while.

"Varina, is there something you want to tell me?"

"I-I don't know." I stood up, holding on to my drink. "I think I'd better go lie down."

"What about the name Jessica . . . does that mean anything to you?"

"Jessica?" I was so very tired. I started down the hallway, toward my room where I could rest. I could barely keep my eyes open. The name Jessica sounded so familiar; nice, like someone I wanted to know.

"Are you all right?" my aunt was asking, coming up behind me.

I nodded, then shook my head, everything growing fuzzy and dim . . . I reached out for the wall to steady myself and I heard a glass falling . . . shattering to the floor . . . then my world went black.

NINE

Darkness sucked me into a black hole of nothing and held me captive. Calm, peaceful feelings lured me to stay awhile, relax under warm blankets, and drift along serene clouds of slumber. I liked this carefree sense of contentment. No stress. No problems. Nothing and no one to worry about.

But something's wrong, a voice hissed to me.

Varina! You have to wake up now! the voice insisted. *Open your eyes and run!*

Why would I want to run anywhere when I could float so freely in this lovely darkness? *Go away,* I told the voice. *I just want to sleep.*

Hurry, before it's too late! Force your eyes open. Now! the voice ordered, and somehow it was familiar; soft, affectionate, someone who cared about me.

Immediately I opened my eyes and saw a slim figure in white standing over me. Aunt Ginny.

Her rich, perfumed scent swirled in the

air and something flashed like silver light-
ning.

Then my loving, gentle Aunt Ginny raised
her hand and aimed a long, deadly needle
directly at me.

TEN

I wanted to jump up and run, but my body wouldn't obey. The drink, I realized! It must have been drugged, because even though my eyes were open, I couldn't move. Like a stuffed doll, I lie helplessly in my own bed, watching the needle slice through the air, then swoosh by my face and toward my arm.

Suddenly, I twisted sideways.

Whoosh! The needle stabbed my pillow.

"Damn," I heard my aunt exclaim. Then she lifted the needle again above my arm . . .

Panic shot through me like a fired flare. And I felt some life leap back into my body. My fingers moved and I managed to utter a hoarse cry.

"Varina!" Aunt Ginny cried in surprise. "You're awake?"

I tried to nod, failed, and simply blinked my eyes.

"I've been so worried about you," she said, sounding distressed. "You suddenly collapsed. Fortunately you were near your room, so I was able to carry you into bed. Poor child, all the anxiety over your uncle has made you ill. Are you feeling better?"

There was only enough strength in me to utter a few words, so I chose them carefully. "W . . . Why . . . nee . . . needle?" I managed to squeak out.

"You mean my syringe?" Her glance swept to a dresser top where she'd set the sharp needle. "Oh, you saw that?"

I answered with a blink.

"Well, I was so worried about you, I had to do something."

I waited, cloudy thoughts whirling in confusion.

"I suppose it must seem odd from your perspective," she said with a thin laugh. "But you passed out so suddenly, I feared you might be seriously ill. So I was going to take a blood sample."

I blinked twice. A blood sample? That seemed strange, but then I couldn't think clearly. My brain wasn't working well; slow and foggy. It was taking a supreme amount of effort just to keep my eyes open. But I was terrified of closing them, unsure of what had happened to me. I remembered wondering if I'd been drugged. And yet Aunt Ginny said I was sick. I felt so strange, unlike any sickness I'd known.

"The syringe wouldn't have hurt," she explained. "I'm trained as a lab technician and have done thousands of blood tests. I only wanted to make sure you were okay."

"I'm . . . okay," I whispered.

"I can see that now. Thank goodness!" She reached down and squeezed my hand. "Losing your father was hard enough for me, I couldn't bear it if I lost you, too."

I nodded, tears filling my eyes at the mention of my father. Instantly, I felt guilty for mistrusting Aunt Ginny; thinking she drugged my drink and tried to harm me. What an ungrateful brat. I was only glad she didn't know my ugly suspicions.

Aunt Ginny bent down to gently pat my cheek. "You rest. You need sleep to gain your strength."

I nodded, enjoying her comforting touch.

She caressed my hair, then pulled my covers snugly over my shoulders. "Tomorrow you can visit your uncle, but tonight just rest. Sleep tight, my sweet Varina."

And then she left.

I dozed off for a while, but didn't sleep tight. Because sometime afterward, I awoke to hear a clatter and rattle at my window.

An intruder was sneaking inside my room!

Eleven

"Chase!" I bolted up. "What are you doing in here?"

"Keep your voice down," he warned, hurrying to my door and peaking out into the hallway. "You don't want her to overhear you."

"Her?" I pushed off covers, glad to find I was still wearing my jeans and a T-shirt. I was even more glad to realize my body was moving normally again. "Do you mean my aunt?"

"If she's really your aunt."

"You are the most suspicious person in the world. I mean, I should be the one disbelieving you. You tell lies about my uncle, insult my aunt, and break into my house." I faced him defiantly. "Give me one reason why I should believe you."

"Because your uncle would want you to," he said gravely. "He'd want me to warn you."

And yet, I thought, Uncle Jim had asked

me to warn Chase and three others. Had my uncle known that someone was going to go after Chase? And what about the break-in at my house? What did that have to do with Chase and the other three people on the list? I could see the list clearly in my mind, the names and addresses. That paper was the only real proof I had of anything.

"How do you know my uncle?"

"When I was little, he was like a father to me. He didn't have a gray hair back then, so he looked different. He used to read stories to me. My favorite was *Where the Wild Things Are.*"

"He read that to me, too," I recalled fondly. "I loved the scary drawings, and the last line was so good. But how could Uncle Jim have been with you when he was with me?"

"He was with both of us, only you were too young to remember." Chase gave a half smile. "Dr. James, that's what I called him, used to thumb wrestle and tell me dumb jokes. A real cool guy. And I thought he was my own private property. That's why I was so mad when the babies came. I was young, but I've been remembering a lot lately. I wanted him all to myself."

"Babies? My uncle is a college professor, not a nanny."

"It's complicated. I'll explain after we get out of here." His tone was low and urgent. "You're not safe here."

"You really expect me to just leave and go to who-knows-where with you?"

"If you're smart."

I stared at him, trying to sort things out. Moonlight from the window made his white hair seem unearthly, and I was reminded of the angel in my dream. She had warned me, too. All these vague warnings, but no solid facts. How could I be in danger?

Maybe Chase had the answers — but I wasn't ready to trust him.

"You still don't believe me," he said with a grim shake of his head. He looked alert suddenly, and tensed. "Did you hear that?"

"What?"

"Your aunt is making a phone call."

I heard nothing except Chase's quick breath and the thundering pound of my own heart. With my door shut, all sounds from the rest of the house were cut off.

Chase rose and went to the door, opening it a crack. He turned back toward me and motioned that I join him. It all seemed pretty weird, but weird was beginning to be the norm.

"Listen," he told me.

I leaned against the wall, listening for any

wisp of conversation, and I did hear a low rumble of my aunt's voice. But I couldn't make out any of her words. How could Chase have heard her through a closed door?

"What's she saying?"

"Quiet. She's talking —" Chase's tone was impatient and anxious, his dark brows narrowed to a frown. "Saying that she has some doubts about 'the girl's identity' but will proceed as planned."

"I didn't hear any of that. How can you?" I demanded, then stopped as the wheels in my brain digested information. "The girl? Does she mean me?"

He nodded, which sent chills through me. And I had to hear for myself. So I pushed past him and cautiously crept down the hallway.

"Varina, don't. Stay back," Chase ordered. But that only made me angry. I'd had enough of being told what to do. This was my house. Aunt Ginny may or may not be my aunt. Whatever the truth was, I would personally find out.

Reaching the living room, I hunched down behind a recliner and saw Aunt Ginny sitting on the couch with a phone to her face. So Chase had been telling the truth.

". . . don't worry," Aunt Ginny said,

kicking off her expensive camel-hair shoes and curling her legs beneath her. "She's giving me no trouble. Such a nice, gullible girl. Very convenient. . . . No, I haven't done the tests yet, although I tried to get a blood sample . . . I'll try again later, but this time I'll make sure she's unconscious. . . . Yes, I'll do the lab work I have the equipment."

I shivered, not liking my aunt's tone at all. The warmth we'd shared while shopping had vanished. In its place was an ice-cold, calculating manner.

Beside me, Chase touched my shoulder as if to comfort me.

". . . not till the afternoon?" Aunt Ginny continued, sounding impatient. "But I am so tired of this pretense. I was not cut out to play the motherly type, although I did buy the most divine shoes today, so it wasn't a total waste. . . . If you insist, but no more kindly Aunt Ginny pretending to mourn some phony brother. I'll simply sedate her again and begin the tests."

Sedate! Tests!

And then I watched Aunt Ginny reach down and lift up a briefcase, which she sat on the coffee table. She spun a combination lock, popping it open. Then she drew out several glass test tubes, plastic gloves, another syringe, and a sharp silver scalpel.

She gave an amused laugh, as if the person on the other end of the phone line said something witty. "Oh, Vic . . . I do miss you . . . hurry here, darling. . . . Yes, it'll be like old times in the lab." She pushed the syringe, a hiss of liquid squirting into the air, and then smiled. "I can't wait to get started. . . ."

"She's going to hang up!" Chase grabbed my arm and roughly pulled me back. "We have to get out of here. *Now!*"

I nodded, and followed him back down the hall to my room. I was numb with fear, unable to get the image of that long sharp scalpel out of my mind. Aunt Ginny meant to use that scalpel on *me*. Tests! As if I were a lab rat!

"You were right about her," I told Chase.

He nodded. "And it's worse than I thought. Did you hear what she called the guy she was talking to?"

I shook my head. All I could remember was that needle, and the cold way she had spoken of me. My father wasn't her brother and everything she'd told me had been a lie. At least I knew that my first instinct about her had been right — she was not my aunt.

"She called him Vic," Chase said, looking

as shaken as I felt. "As in Dr. Mansfield Victor."

"The man who . . ." I began.

And Chase finished, "Killed my parents."

My mouth fell open. "That means she's the accomplice!"

Chase nodded, and I knew then that I had to trust him.

So when he asked me to leave with him, I didn't hesitate. I grabbed my purse, packed a few clothes and precious belongings in a suitcase, and left.

Twelve

It was dark, the moon shrouded in misty clouds and the streets as silent as death. Any fatigue I had felt before had vanished; fear and adrenaline gave me strength.

Chase led me a few blocks away to a midsize blue truck with a shell. "This is where I've been staying. It's not much, but it's home for now."

"You're living in a *truck?*"

"It's easier and cheaper, until I figure things out."

"By things, you mean me?"

"One of them." His gray-blue eyes shone with seriousness. "But there are others."

"I'm tired of all these cryptic answers. I want you to be straight with me," I insisted.

"Yeah, you should know the truth." He nodded, car keys dangling from his fingers. "Get in, and let's put some miles between us and that phony aunt of yours."

"She is a phony," I said sadly, mourning the "mother" I almost had. Betrayal was keen and bitter. And she'd called me gullible . . . I would never trust so easily again.

I slipped into the passenger seat of the small truck and locked the door behind me. It seemed strange to be with an unknown older guy in his car, one of the big don'ts for nice girls. And yet this wasn't a romantic thing, it was life or death. Although I had to admit there was something compelling about Chase. I didn't fully trust him, and yet I felt a strange fascination. I definitely wanted to know more about him.

Chase started the car, switched on the heater, and drove away from my once peaceful neighborhood. Glancing over at him, I waited for his explanation, noticing his tight grip on the steering wheel and strained expression.

After a few miles, he turned to me. "Okay, ask away. I know you're bursting with questions."

"You're really going to be honest?"

"You got it. Total truth."

I leaned against the leather seat, glancing through the window at the outside world of streetlights and neon signs, a world that seemed long ago and out of reach. Safety and normalness was yesterday, and I wondered what today would bring.

"You said you knew me as a baby," I

began slowly. "Tell me about that first."

"Well . . ." He tapped his fingers on the steering wheel, pausing for a red light. "I guess I'll just tell you what I know, which isn't everything. My memories are still sketchy."

"Too bad you don't have my memory. I never have to study for tests. Once I read something, I don't forget it."

"Lucky you. I had to cram like crazy just to graduate high school. And I was enjoying my college classes, only that's over now. Everything changed with the fire and finding out . . ." He stopped suddenly, scowled, then continued. "Anyway, it's taken me a while to piece together the truth. At first I didn't believe it."

"Didn't believe what?"

"That I was . . . uh . . . different. When I was very young, I lived on the ocean in a big boat with three scientists. I don't know a lot about them, but I called them Dr. James, Dr. Hart, and Dr. Victor."

"My uncle Jim was Dr. James?"

He nodded.

"And Dr. Victor?" I choked out. "The man who tried to kill you?"

"Yeah. But that's later in the story. On the boat, I was happy. Dr. Hart was like my mother and Dr. James was like my father.

They were great to me. Only Dr. Victor was different, arguing a lot with the other doctors and short-tempered with me. I learned to hide whenever he was around."

"Where were your real parents?" I wanted to know.

"I thought Dr. James and Dr. Hart *were* my parents. That's why I was so mad when the babies came."

"Yeah, you mentioned the babies before."

"Four babies. They cried a lot and the doctors spent more time with them than me. I was so jealous. I liked being the only kid on our boat, and hated having to share."

In my mind I imagined a large ship floating aimlessly at sea, white-jacketed doctors moving through corridors, and a little boy with pale hair frowning at four cribs. There was a man in a white coat who yelled at the blond boy, lifting his hand, reaching out to . . .

I shook my head to clear my wild imagination. Then I asked, "But why would anyone raise children on a boat?"

"We weren't normal children. We were scientific experiments," he said with a chilling calmness.

"What are you talking about?" If I'd been the one driving, my shock would have sent us straight into oncoming traffic.

"Like I said, my memories are vague. I was three or four when the babies came, and turning five when everything changed."

"How old are you now?"

"Eighteen. Which would make the babies fifteen by now." He blew out a tired sigh. "The doctors never called us by normal names, we were numbers to them. Although when Dr. James and Dr. Hart called me 'Six,' I knew they loved me like a son. I was never just a number to them."

"But why experiment on little kids?" The idea was terrifying and made me think of the syringe in Aunt Ginny's hand — like something out of a horror movie.

We had pulled into a twenty-four-hour grocery store lit up with neon lights, and parked among other cars as if this were an ordinary trip to buy groceries. When the engine dimmed to a low hum and the truck stopped, Chase turned to me solemnly.

I wondered if he was going to hold my hand or caress my face. For a quick moment, I even wished he would, which was totally nuts.

"Varina, this is hard to explain." He spoke softly, his dark brows arched over his sincere gray-blue eyes.

"What?" My pulse quickened as I met his gaze.

"I didn't know the truth until I overheard Dr. Victor talking about me."

"The night he burned your home?"

He nodded, misery etched into his rugged face. And I wished I could smooth away his pain. "I always knew I wasn't like the other kids. I didn't have real parents and I didn't know much about my past. Then I was in foster homes, some bad and some good, until the Johnsons took me in when I was eight. They didn't ask me for much, just my respect and love. They were the best . . ."

He stopped, looked away, then returned to face me. "Anyway, life was good. My dad taught me all about the outdoors. We went hiking, fishing, pheasant hunting, and rock climbing." The dark cloud around him seemed to lift, real affection for his foster parents shining through, and for a moment he was like any normal teen guy.

"Rock climbing? Sounds cool."

"Yeah, things were great. Dad had a few health problems, but that didn't stop our outdoor trips. Although when I hit thirteen, life got kind of weird. I noticed my hearing had changed."

"How?"

"I could hear things others couldn't. And by fifteen, I could hear conversations through walls and long distances away."

"Like when you heard Aunt Ginny's phone call," I said.

"Yeah. Only this talent made me freak. Even my parents gave me weird looks, like they were uneasy about me. And they warned me not to tell anyone. So I kept quiet, things were okay again, until . . . last week I woke up, it was late at night, and I heard this man talking about me."

"If this is too hard, you don't have to tell me." I could see his grief.

"No. You have to know," he said harshly. "I looked out my window and saw a car with someone inside. I heard this guy talking, he had a soft Spanish accent that sounded harsh when he talked about killing me."

"Dr. Victor?"

"Right. With my unusual hearing, I heard every word he said. He wanted all traces of me erased because of what I was."

I raised my brows, a silent question.

"I wasn't just raised on the boat. I was created there."

"Like a test-tube baby?" I knew some couples used doctors to help them become parents. It was very common, nothing to be embarrassed about.

"You're partly right. I was a test-tube baby, but more than that." He took a deep breath. "I only have one parent, not two."

"Huh?"

"I'm a clone."

"A . . . a *what?*"

"And there's more." He reached out, his coarse fingers touching my hands. "Varina, you were one of the four babies on the boat — which makes you a clone, too."

Thirteen

I could tell Chase expected me to freak out. When I started to smile, his jaw dropped in astonishment.

"You do believe me, don't you?" he asked.

"I believe you were on that boat, and I guess I believe Uncle Jim was one of the doctors. I mean, I know he's fascinated by genetic research. Cloning on animals is a fact, so it makes sense it can be done with humans, too."

"That doesn't upset you?"

"Of course not. My uncle is a scientist, I've spent my entire life listening to him discuss theories and research."

"So you don't mind being a clone?"

"That's where you're wrong." I continued smiling. "You may be a clone, but I definitely am not. I can't possibly be one of those four babies."

"Why?" he demanded.

"Because you said those four kids would be fifteen this year. But I'm older than that.

My birthday is next week and I'm turning sixteen."

"Sixteen?"

"Next week. Hmm . . . maybe that's why Aunt Ginny — or whoever she really is — seemed confused about my age."

"Her real name is Geneva," Chase told me. "That's what the guy on the phone called her."

"You heard that?"

He nodded. "Being a scientific experiment has its advantages. You might have an unusual power, too."

"*If* I were a clone, but I already told you I'm not." My head ached and suddenly things began to make sense. "No wonder Geneva insisted I was only fifteen. She thinks I'm a clone! But she's wrong! I have pictures of my real parents and Uncle Jim has told me a lot about my mother."

"I remember the red-haired girl baby," Chase said, clearly trying to sort this out. "And when I saw you with Dr. James, I guessed you were that girl. Dr. James didn't have any children of his own. It just made sense."

"Well, you guessed wrong." I gave a heavy sigh and stared into Chase's gray-blue eyes, mysterious and compelling. Too bad I'd disappointed him, not being a clone. Not that I wanted to be a science experiment! But it would have given us something in common.

"I'm sorry," I murmured. "It must be hard finding this sort of thing out."

"You have no idea." He bit his lip and looked so fierce for a moment that I felt afraid. But then he smiled, and I relaxed.

"I don't know much about clones," I admitted. "Except it sounds creepy. I don't think I'd like it."

"No, you wouldn't. Especially when your DNA is . . . well, you just wouldn't like it. And knowing where you came from, what you may become, can be even worse."

"What's that supposed to mean?"

"Nothing." He shrugged. "If you're not a clone, you don't have to worry. But then where are the four babies . . . I mean . . . teenagers?"

"How should I know?"

"Because your uncle knows! I overheard Dr. Victor say that Dr. James took the babies."

"My uncle took four babies?"

"It happened thirteen years ago. Didn't he ever mention other kids to you? Three girls and a boy?"

"No. This is way too bizarre. But what about that woman doctor you mentioned, Dr. Hart? Maybe she has the kids."

"No. She was shot saving me and the babies." Chase's voice dropped sadly. "Dr. James, your uncle Jim, has all the answers. He must have told you something. We need to find the other clones before Dr. Victor finds them."

"What does he want with them?"

"The same thing he wanted with me."

"No! But . . . but he tried to kill you . . . and he did kill . . ."

"Go ahead, say it Varina. Dr. Victor killed my parents. I can't bring them back, but I can stop him from hurting anyone else." His voice grew fierce. "Those four kids are in danger."

"And you, Chase." I almost reached out to squeeze his hand, but stopped myself. "You're in danger, too."

"I can take care of myself, but those kids don't know someone is after them." He hit his fist against the steering wheel. "There has to be some way to warn them. But they could be anywhere. I don't even know their names. It's hopeless."

"Maybe not."

While Chase stared in surprise, I reached into my pocket and drew out the folded paper. Then I showed him the four names that included his own.

FOURTEEN

I absolutely refused.

"No way, not on your life, never in a zillion years," I told Chase firmly. "Giving you the list was one thing, but I am not, I repeat not, going with you to San Francisco."

"You can't back out now."

"Watch me."

"Use your head and think! These people are deadly!" Frustration tinged his face red, and I felt a jolt of fear. There was something so raw and rugged about Chase, as if violence seethed inside him.

I drew back, my hand clutching the car door handle. "I didn't ask to be part of this."

"Neither did I." Anguish shone from his eyes and he added in a low voice, "I need your help."

"Uncle Jim needs me, too. I can't leave him. Please drop me off at the hospital." I folded my arms resolutely across my chest. "Then you can warn Allison Beaumont."

"Allison won't believe me any more than

you did at first. But if you come with me, we can convince her."

"Me? I wouldn't know what to say. I mean, you don't just go up to someone and say, 'Excuse me, but you were created in a lab and only have one parent.' Besides, what if we're wrong?"

"How could we be wrong? Your uncle told you to warn the people on the list, including me. Allison, Sandee, and Eric must also be clones. And if the list wasn't torn, we'd know about the other one. It all makes sense."

"But what if this list has nothing to do with Geneva or Dr. Victor? Maybe the names mean something else. They could be former students of Uncle Jim's."

"Or former experiments," Chase said with a wry twist of his mouth. "Like me. And they probably have some freak power, too."

"You really think so?"

"The experiment on the boat did more than clone us, because my hearing is so incredible. The others might have super hearing, too."

"Wow. You think so?" For the first time since learning about this whole clone thing, I felt a stirring of curiosity. Science had always intrigued me and I'd often watched quietly while Uncle Jim worked with test tubes and chemicals. I'd never seen him experiment on anything living, and the concept of cloning blew me away. Playing God with DNA . . . I couldn't help but be fascinated.

Still, I couldn't just take off and go to San Francisco on a wild clone chase. Not with Uncle Jim in the hospital.

"Varina, it isn't safe for you to stay in Liberty Hills," Chase said, his elbow resting on the steering wheel as he faced me. "That bogus aunt of yours will be after you. She thinks you're one of the clones."

"But I'm not!"

"She doesn't know that — and neither does Dr. Victor. The two of them are in this together."

"Then you're in more danger than I am. Go to the police and ask them for protection," I said wearily, just wanting to go back to my normal life.

"Impossible."

"Why?"

"It just is," he said angrily. "Don't you get it, Varina? I have no proof, just stuff I overheard. Besides, Dr. Victor isn't after me anymore. He doesn't know I escaped the fire."

"He thinks you're dead?"

"Probably." Chase nodded with grim satisfaction. "And I would be if I hadn't climbed out of a back window to follow him. But he was already driving away, and when I started to go back . . ." His voice broke. "There was an explosion and I was knocked to the ground by the blast. I didn't come to till the fire trucks arrived . . . but it was all over by then."

I nodded sympathetically, feeling his sorrow.

"And now Dr. Victor is after the others," Chase went on bitterly. "That's why he searched your house, trying to track them down. Dr. Victor wants all the clones dead."

"Then why didn't Aunt Gin— I mean, Geneva — try to kill me? If she thought I was a clone . . ."

"I don't have all the answers!" he snapped. "You think this is fun and games for me? My whole life blew up, and I couldn't stop it. Suddenly there were flames and then boom . . ." He ran his hand over his eyes and groaned. "So I can't go back . . . only forward."

"I'm so sorry. I wish I could help."

"You can."

"No, I can't! This is so wild. People don't go around killing other people without a reason. Why now, after so many years?"

"For scientific research, or maybe Dr. Victor is just a total psycho trying to erase his past. Messing around with clones and DNA could get him in big trouble."

"After thirteen years?"

"The only thing I know for sure is he's bad news." Chase's tone was fierce and his jaw tightened. "Geneva is, too. And I'm not gonna let them hurt anyone else."

I remembered the sharp needle coming at me in the dark. Why a blood sample? For some kind of wacko experiment? And the scalpel, test tubes, and other medical equipment . . . what had those been for? To poke and prod me like a biology experiment?

Horrible. Thank goodness Chase had warned me in time. And I couldn't ignore his suspicions. I wasn't the product of some sicko scientific experiment, but unless I could convince Geneva of this fact, I was in danger, too.

Still that didn't change my anxiety for my uncle. No matter how much I wanted to help Chase find Allison, I couldn't abandon my uncle.

"I have to go to the hospital," I insisted, knowing I was being stubborn but seeing no choice. "If Uncle Jim is better, he can help us."

"Yeah, he could. He knows more about Dr. Victor and Geneva than we do."

"And don't forget the missing clone. The

paper is torn, so my uncle is the only one who can find that kid."

"Which would make things easier for us," Chase admitted reluctantly. "But it's risky showing up in a public place."

"What about the risk to Uncle Jim?" I asked, a new fear gripping me. "I mean, if he knows so much, won't Dr. Victor be after him, too?"

"I doubt it. Your uncle's in a busy hospital with lots of people around. And he's a valuable source of information for Dr. Victor, so he should be safe. We're the moving targets." Chase scowled, then roughly reached forward and twisted the car key so the engine roared back to life. "But you win."

"You'll take me to the hospital?"

"Yeah." He pursed his lips and gave me a dark look. "I just hope we aren't making a big mistake."

FIFTEEN

Night had slipped into early dawn and low shifting clouds hinted of rain. Entering the hospital was like slipping into a quiet cocoon where uniformed workers moved through the halls in hushed activity. Other employees sat behind desks or in cubicles, speaking in low conversation or busily filling out forms, while visitors read or dozed in the lobby.

Chase and I walked side by side, not speaking, but bristling with alertness. I sensed his simmering anxiety, his desire to be somewhere else, yet I knew I was doing the right thing. I couldn't leave town and desert Uncle Jim. What if he asked for me?

"I'll wait here," Chase said in a low voice, "while you find out about your uncle." He stopped, half-hidden between a large green fern and a wall.

I nodded, then walked over to the reception desk. I was disappointed not to see Nurse Burns. But then she had a family, a full life of her own, and couldn't be expected to live at the hospital. Besides, if she'd been here and asked how I was getting along with my aunt, I'd have to lie to her.

"Your uncle is in room 233B," a perky male nurse wearing one gold earring informed me.

"How is he?"

The nurse consulted a chart, then shook his head sadly. "His condition is stable, but critical. He's still in a coma. You'll have to discuss it with his doctor for more details."

"Oh, no!" I cried softly, fighting off tears. I had counted on Uncle Jim getting better soon. I needed him so badly. "Can . . . Can I see him?"

"That's not my call." A curt shrug of his shoulders. "You'll need to check with the doctor."

"But —"

Behind me, I heard a footstep and then felt Chase's strong hand gently touch my shoulder. Turning, I read concern in his gaze, and that touched me. He acted tough and indifferent, but he was worried about my uncle, too. That made me feel better.

"We'll find him ourselves," Chase whispered. "Come on."

"Okay."

We left the lobby area and followed signs, going up to the second floor, and locating numbered patient rooms.

"Rooms 240 to 260 are that direction," I said, "so we'll go the other way. He's in room 233B."

"Yeah," he agreed, following me.

We reached Room 231A, when suddenly Chase grabbed me and yanked me around a corner. "Out of sight!" he ordered.

"What?" I pressed tightly against the wall, looking around in quick fear. And then I saw the slender dark-haired woman whose sharp beige pumps clicked noisily as she moved.

Geneva! And she stood beside a thin bald Hispanic man in a doctor's coat, with narrow gold-framed glasses perched on his beaklike nose. His brown eyes narrowed in a fierce scowl as he spoke to Geneva.

"That's Dr. Victor," Chase told me, looking suddenly pale and angry.

"Oh, no! What are they doing here? Do you think they're planning to hurt Uncle Jim?"

"No." Chase tilted his head to one side as if listening. "Not yet."

"Thank goodness."

"Dr. Victor says they want Jim alive since he's the only one who might have the information."

"What information?"

"Shh! I can't hear —"

"I thought you had this super hearing," I snapped. It felt good to get a little angry, better than being scared.

"I'm hearing plenty," he said in a low tone. "And your uncle isn't our big worry now. They're after you."

I gave a low gasp. "Me!"

"Yeah. Geneva says she knows you'll come to see your uncle. That's why they're here. And Dr. Victor is ticked off at Geneva, accusing her of being careless and letting you escape."

I heard nothing, of course. Chase's hearing was truly amazing . . .

"What else?"

"Geneva insists she wasn't careless. She doesn't know why 'the girl' left, but it won't happen next time. She mentioned a stronger sedative . . . needles . . . blood samples . . ." Chase was quiet for a moment, frowning.

When he shuddered, I knew he'd overhead something horrible. I touched his arm and gave him a questioning look. But he simply looked away, not meeting my gaze.

"Chase, tell me."

"You don't want to know, believe me."

I believed him, and my stomach twisted in knots.

Chase listened for a while longer, and I waited in grim silence. I stayed behind the wall, out of sight, and safe for the moment.

Finally, Chase leaned toward me, his finger to his lips. "This is worse than I guessed."

"What do you mean?"

"They plan to take care of you — don't ask — and then go after the other clones."

"But they don't have the list."

"They found a note when they searched your house that mentioned 'Allison' and a San Francisco address."

"No!" I choked out, too loud, because an elderly woman passing gave me a startled look. This was not a safe place, I realized instantly. But was any place safe?

"Varina, I know you don't want to leave your uncle, but you have to."

I nodded, my throat thickening with emotion. Poor Uncle Jim, battered, bruised, and in a coma. I wanted to be with him, and yet I didn't dare, not with the enemy watching his door. I could cry out for help if Dr. Victor and Geneva grabbed me, but they'd probably say I was a mixed-up kid and they were trying to take care of me. I already knew how well Geneva could play the kindly "Aunt Ginny." And adults believed other adults. They seldom believed teenagers.

I couldn't go home and yet I couldn't stay

at the hospital. Sure, I had some friends, but they belonged with my old life in Oregon. And my hopes for a friendship with Starr had long since slipped away. I had no one . . . except Chase.

Then I thought of Allison. She needed help, too. If she really was one of the clones, now fifteen years old, she was probably living a normal life, trying to fit in with other teenagers, and perhaps noticing that something was different about her. Maybe she could hear through walls like Chase. But unusual hearing wouldn't protect her from Dr. Victor and Geneva.

Only Chase and I could protect Allison and the others.

So I gave one last fearful glance down the hall where Dr. Victor and Geneva barred the door to my uncle, and sighed sadly, finally ready to leave for San Francisco with Chase.

But as I stepped back, Geneva suddenly looked up, down the corridor, and directly at me!

"Oh, no! I blew it!" I cried, grabbing Chase's hand and beginning to run. "She saw me! I'm sorry!"

"We'll be okay," he spoke through quick breaths. "Just keep moving. Don't look back."

I did as he said, hurrying swiftly through the hallway, struggling to keep up with Chase. I ignored the surprised looks from people we passed and just stayed focused on getting away. Through the lobby, out the automatic doors, and into the parking lot.

"Are they . . . still after . . . us?" I asked.

"Yes! Hurry, Varina!"

No argument there. I hurried, ducking with him around cars and shrubbery, heading for his truck, which had been parked in a distant corner. Once there, Chase unlocked the doors, and we scrambled inside.

He turned the key and the car roared to life.

I yanked my seat belt on, feeling the car rush forward, hearing tires squeal, and smelling burned rubber as we ripped around a corner . . . fleeing the hospital.

Only then did I look back.

And I saw two figures who angrily watched us drive away.

Sixteen

I hadn't been to San Francisco in two years, when my uncle had taken me to Golden Gate Park and Ghiradelli Square. We'd also shopped at trendy, rustic Pier 39, which was fun, despite the sudden downpour that left us huddling under cover.

As Chase drove, I pretended to be watching out the window, noticing the continuous panorama of sprawling upscale communities, occasional hulking factories, and glimpses of gray-blue bay. But all I could think about was Allison. If Dr. Victor and Geneva had her address, she was in big trouble. We just had to find her first.

Glancing at Chase, I could tell he was worried, too. His jaw was clenched with purpose and I was getting intense vibes from him; that unusual blend of dark and light. I knew he was my ally, and yet something primitive about him still bothered me. Or maybe I was bothered by my growing attraction to him.

I wanted to understand, to know the secrets my sixth sense hinted at, so I faced Chase and said the first thing that popped into my mind. "Thanks for, you know, everything. You were right about it being risky to go to the hospital. I messed up."

"It'll be okay. They saw you, but I don't think they got a clear look at me. It's better if they assume I'm dead."

"I guess so." I let out a heavy sigh. "I think my heart is still pounding."

"Just sit back and rest until we get there."

"How long will that be?"

"About a half hour. I checked the map and Allison lives in an older, mega-bucks neighborhood. Telling her isn't going to be easy."

"You'd know," I said simply. Then I paused and asked, "What's it like, Chase? Being a clone?"

The look he gave me was sharp and severe. "I haven't sprouted three heads and pointy ears. I'm not any different than before."

"But you can hear, like, a zillion times better than most people. And you were . . . uh . . . created. You have to feel different."

"I'm not a freak, if that's what you mean."

"No . . . No . . . I-I didn't mean —"

"So what did you mean?" he demanded.

"Not that!" I tried to explain. "You're smart, kind, and brave. You probably saved my life, and I'm grateful. Being a clone is interesting. You shouldn't be ashamed."

"I'm not ashamed." He flipped on his turning signal, shifted sharply into the right lane. His knuckles on the steering wheel were white and his arms rigid.

"You're a living miracle, Chase. And your hearing is incredible. Think of the breakthrough for hearing-impaired people this could lead to. If science can create you, then even more wondrous things are possible."

"Come off it, Varina. This isn't a wondrous thing, it's a curse. I never asked to be different . . . to be a copy of someone else."

"A copy of who?" I asked, my seat belt straining as I leaned toward him.

He shot a dangerous look at me. "Don't ask . . . *ever.*"

"Don't you wonder about him? Or do you already know?"

"It doesn't matter," he growled. "My DNA isn't who I am."

"It partly is."

"Not the part that matters. I'm more than a science experiment. And I just want to be me. You'd feel the same way in my place."

"No. It would be like being a twin, not so alone."

"Yeah, right," he scoffed. "Family means a lot to you. Look how quick you were to believe that Geneva was your aunt, just because you wanted a mother figure. I was watching your house when you came back with all those shopping bags. You were totally suckered in by her auntie dearest act."

I cringed, feeling again a stinging stab of betrayal. I *had* trusted Aunt Ginny. But I knew better now.

"Okay, so I do care about family. But even if I found out I *was* a clone, that wouldn't mean my uncle didn't love me. Nothing would change in my life."

"Everything changes," Chase spoke grimly.

"But some changes are for the better," I pointed out, sorry for all the sadness in his life and wishing I could make it better. And I wondered if he ever dated younger girls. . . .

We were driving over the Bay Bridge, which rose high and then dipped low into San Francisco. Boats dotted the water below, and off in the distance I saw the dark island of Alcatraz.

"We'll be there soon," Chase said quietly. "We need a plan so we don't scare Allison."

"Good idea."

"We can pretend to be doing a survey."

"What kind?" I asked.

"You come up with something." He slowed as the traffic merged and he entered a one-way street. "Make it personal, so Allison will tell us about herself."

"A survey on teen likes and dislikes."

"Add something about family, too," Chase said. "I bet she's adopted, or a foster kid like I was."

"That makes sense. Maybe my uncle traveled around, leaving you and the other kids with different adoption agencies to protect them."

"I was left in Nevada, and they live in Texas, Colorado, and California. Too bad we don't know where the last kid is."

"A girl, right?" I guessed. "Since you thought I was her."

"There were three girls and one boy. Also, me. We didn't have real names, just numbers back then. Of course now everyone has a name. The boy in Texas is Eric Prince."

"Texas and Colorado are so far away." I felt a sense of frustration. "How will we get there?"

"We'll figure it out. I have a credit card and some cash, but I'm not rolling in money, so airfare is out of the question. Unless you have a big stash of cash handy?" He gave me a hopeful look.

"Not even. I have a savings account, but

that's for college and Uncle Jim keeps the passbook in his office. After the break-in, I don't know if it's still there." I felt my stomach rumble with hunger and realized money could become a problem. We'd need to buy food and gas. Running away was complicated.

The truck slowed for a passing streetcar brimming with tourists, then we left the downtown area, where the traffic thinned and elegant Victorian homes multiplied, standing tall and close in bright rainbow hues.

I reached for my purse, which I'd tossed on the floor, and pulled out a paper and pen. What sort of survey questions should I ask Allison? I'd start out with fun topics like favorite music groups, sports teams, and movie stars. Did she play a musical instrument, compete in a sport? These things would draw her out, gain her trust, and then we could ask more serious questions — like if she had any baby pictures, odd memories of a boat, or could hear remote conversations through solid walls.

We'd be lucky if she didn't slam the door in our faces.

Frowning, I put away the paper and pen. And when I glanced up, I realized we were slowing down and parking in front of an impressive, towering lime-green Victorian mansion. A wrought-iron fence protectively circled the home, its spiky Gothic gate barring the way; an un-welcome mat for visitors.

Chase shut the engine off, glancing over at me with a half smile. "You ready to tackle the Clone Zone?"

"Clone Zone, huh?" I grinned, surprised by his sudden flash of humor. And I realized that before tragedy struck him, he had been just an average guy who laughed at corny jokes, enjoyed outdoor adventures, and made plans for his future.

"This is some awesome place," Chase was saying as he stepped out of the truck. "But how will we get in?"

I shut my door, surveying the forbidding gate, and wondering what sort of life Allison lived inside this pale green fortress. "We better dump the survey plan."

"Yeah." He nodded, rubbing his chin thoughtfully. "You'd have to know someone or have an appointment to get in there. So you should just pretend to be a friend of Allison's."

"Me? What about you?"

"If her family has this much security, they aren't going to let me near a fifteen-year-old girl. But you're close to Allison's age. You can bluff your way in."

"I'm not good at lying. Whenever I try, I end up in worse trouble than ever," I said ruefully.

"You can handle it." He chuckled, coming around and giving me a gentle push. "Go get her."

"Easy for you to say." I felt my cheeks blushing, startled by the light touch of his hands on my back. Only a casual touch, yet somehow it was much more. And I was pleased he trusted me to find Allison. I wouldn't let him down.

So I faced this new challenge, noticing a small brass plate affixed to the gate. PACIFIC PALACE FOR YOUNG LADIES. Hey, this wasn't Allison's home — it was her school. Instead of stern, aristocratic parents to deal with, now I would be facing a headmistress — which made me think of the scary headmistress in a favorite childhood book, *Matilda*.

Not a very hopeful situation.

If only I had more information on Allison. How could I pretend to be her friend if I didn't even know what she looked like? I only knew her age and her unusual past.

There was a button below the brass plate by the gate, and I lifted my hand, poised to push. Only I hesitated, glanced back at

Chase, who sat relaxed with his feet propped on the dash in his truck. "Like he's gonna be any help," I murmured.

Chase raised his head and then waved his hand, giving me a thumbs-up. I couldn't help but grin. I'd forgotten about his keen hearing . . . which was kind of reassuring in a weird way.

I returned my gaze to the button. *Ye who enter, tread carefully,* I thought to myself.

Okay, I'll be careful.

A flash of movement caught my attention, and through the wrought-iron bars I saw a tall figure wearing blue coveralls, a paint-splotched cap, a baggy work belt laden with tools, and carrying a long metal ladder. Hmmm . . . maybe that guy could answer a few basic questions about Allison.

Yet before I could call out, the guy had propped the ladder against the building and started climbing. He stopped at a second-story window and reached for his hammer. If I called out suddenly, I might startle him. He'd fall, probably get knocked out with his own hammer, and with all the ambulances and excitement I'd never be able to find out anything about Allison.

Uncertainly, I looked back at the button on the gate. Stop stalling, Varina, I urged myself. Just push it. A brief touch of my finger and someone would come to the gate . . . only then what?

"You selling something?"

"Selling? Me?" I squealed, whirling around to face two girls about my age dressed alike in navy blue skirts with plaid vests over prim white blouses. One girl wore her thick brunette hair pulled back in a neat ponytail and the other had bright beads woven into a web of wild black braids.

"Who else would we be talking to?" The braids girl giggled and nudged her friend. "Francie and me —"

"Francie and I," the other girl corrected in a lofty tone. "Don't forget Mrs. Manchester's lessons."

"Like I could!" Another giggle. "Proper young ladies always use perfect English. Ain't that right?"

"Darn straight, Reanna!"

They both burst into peals of laughter while I stood there on the pavement uncomfortably shifting my legs.

"Well . . . I was just . . . uh . . . looking for someone."

"Who?" they both asked, instantly curious.

"A friend." I took a deep breath and spit it out before I lost my courage. "Her name's Allison."

"Allison Beaumont?" Reanna asked with a wrinkle of her nose as if she wasn't thrilled to say the name. "Oh, her."

"Allison's okay and all," Francie quickly spoke, with a warning look at Reanna. "I mean, her family is like rolling in moola and major players in Seattle's elite crowd. Oh, but since you're her friend, you know that."

"Of course." I gave my best imitation of a ladylike smile. "Although I haven't seen Allison in a long time. She's, uh, probably changed a lot."

"She's still skinny as a pencil, if that's what you mean," Francie said with a frown down at own her thick waist.

"And her fashion IQ is minus ten," Reanna added. "I keep telling Allison to cut and style all that long dark blond hair, or maybe weave in some gold highlights, but does she listen?"

"Never," Francie answered with a shake of her head.

"Sounds like the same old Allison." I smiled again. "Uh, can you take me to her?"

Reanna and Francie exchanged amused glances and then giggled as if enjoying a private joke.

"Allison is here all right," Francie said.

"Come on in with us," Reanna invited, whipping out a card key and inserting it into a slot I hadn't noticed before. The gate swooshed to life and opened.

"Will you take me to Allison's room?"

"She's not there. She's hanging around involved in one of her projects." Francie met Reanna's gaze again and they started laughing. Francie swept her hands, gesturing to the towering building and spacious well-groomed grounds. "We've got some phone calls to make, so you're on your own."

"But-But how will I find Allison?"

"That's your problem. We've got better things to do." Reanna turned to Francie, waved a paper with numbers on it, then whispered. If Chase were here, he'd know what they said, but I couldn't hear a word. Although from the way their eyes sparkled, cheeks blushed, and they practically drooled, I knew they were hot on the trail of BOYS in capital letters.

Glancing around uncertainly, I followed the two girls up steep cement steps. Still giggling, Reanna and Francie burst through elegant stained-glass double doors, already forgetting I existed, and disappeared inside.

Now it was my turn to enter, but I moved forward slowly. At least I was empowered with new knowledge about Allison. She was thin, with long dark blond hair, and was involved in some unknown project. Okay, now all I had to do was find her.

I reached out to open the door, when suddenly I heard someone shout out urgently, *"Stop! Don't go in there!"*

SEVENTEEN

Whirling around, I saw the guy from the ladder, climbing down and hurrying over to me. As he moved, his tool belt clanged and swayed from his narrow hips.

"Wait!" he called, his voice surprisingly soft.

And then he reached up and lifted off his cap, spilling out a stream of dark blond hair.

Not a guy at all!

"So why were you asking about me?"

My mouth fell open and I stared up at this tall thin girl. "Allison?"

"Yes. I heard you asking those hoochies about me. Why? Did my mother send you? Because if she did, you can just turn around and leave right now."

"No! I don't even know your mother."

"And you wouldn't want to! So what do you want?"

"To help you," I said sincerely.

"Then pick up a hammer and get to work."

"Not that kind of help."

"Can't blame me for trying," she said with a chuckle, not in the gossipy way Reanna and Francie had, but with friendly amusement. Looking closer at her, I realized she was knock-'em-in-the-head-with-a-hammer gorgeous. Her face was smooth, her chocolate-brown eyes wide with long lashes, and her lips were full and bow-shaped. Not even the crumpled heavy overalls could hide her natural beauty.

So why was she trying to hide it?

"Allison, can we go somewhere quiet and talk?"

"About what?"

"Uh . . . something important. You're . . . you are . . ." I sucked in brisk air, trying to think of the right words, and merely exhaled a heavy sigh. "I don't know how to say this."

"Say what?" She leaned toward me, her brow furrowing. "Who are you, anyway?"

"Varina Fergus."

"Never heard of you. But as long as you aren't one of the snooty-nosed pals of my mother's, you're okay with me. Hey, you want to hold my ladder so I can finish fixing the windowsill?"

"Why are *you* fixing a window?"

"Why not?" she returned defiantly. "Just because I live at this stuffy girls' school doesn't mean I have to dress like a fashion queen and sit around sipping tea. I happen to like carpentry, and I'm good at it."

"That's great."

"You really think so?" She sounded pleased.

"Sure. If you're good at something, you should go for it."

"You definitely aren't a friend of Mother's," she said with a chuckle. "Mother would be horrified if she saw me now. Actually, most of the teachers would, too, which is why I tried to cover up." She tucked her hair back under her cap, then gave me a puzzled look. "So why are you here?"

"I know this must seem weird and all, but you're in danger. I came to warn you."

"Yeah." She laughed, clearly not taking me seriously. "In danger of being seriously bored. If you've come to take me away from this dull Pacific Prison for Prissy Princesses, just say the word. I'm outta here."

"Really?" I couldn't believe what I was hearing. This was too good to be true. Maybe I could skip the whole clone talk and convince her to go somewhere safe with Chase and me.

"I'd rather spend my time doing worthwhile stuff, like volunteer work," Allison added, with a sharp pounding of her hammer on the window frame. "Last month I helped build a home for a family of five."

"Wow! That's way cool. I never even thought of doing stuff like that."

"You should," she said sincerely. "It makes you feel good, simple as that. It's like finding out who I really am."

"I think there's more to find out." I bit my tongue, liking her more than I'd expected, and hating having to upset her. "Allison, I wasn't kidding about your being in danger."

"Real danger?" she asked doubtfully as she climbed down and faced me.

"Very real. People have already been hurt." I frowned. "You probably won't believe me, but these bad people will be after you next."

"That's crazy."

"This is so hard to explain. You have no reason to trust me, but you have to. My uncle had your name and address on a paper . . . he was attacked and he asked me to warn the people on the list. It sounds insane just hearing myself say this, so you must really think I'm nuts."

"Yeah." She nodded, her expression growing somber. "But I've learned not to judge people too quickly. Go on."

"You're fifteen years old, right?"

"Yeah. I turned fifteen in August."

"That fits," I said, relieved. "And do you know much about your birth? Do you have baby pictures?"

"What does my birth have to do with this?"

"Everything."

"Now you're scaring me." She pushed a loose strand of blond hair back under her cap and frowned. "What's this about?"

"I have a friend who's waiting outside in his truck, and he could explain this better," I said, afraid when I told her the truth she would dismiss me.

"Maybe this is a kidnap plot, and you're trying to lure me outside so your friend can grab me."

"No!" I exclaimed, horrified. "I would never . . . I really am trying to warn you. You're in danger, but not from me. The same bad people are after Chase and me."

"Chase?"

"My friend," I added in a soft voice, knowing Chase was probably listening. "He likes to act dangerous, but really he's a softie. You can trust him."

"Funny thing is, I believe you. Which makes no sense at all." She rubbed her forehead, some grime leaving a dark slash above her brows. "Okay, this is probably totally wrong, but let's go out and I'll listen to your friend."

"Great!" I almost jumped for joy. "You won't be sorry."

"I hope not," she said, her hand resting comfortably on the hammer in her work belt. "I may look like a weakling, but you'd be surprised at how well I can defend myself. This had better not be a scam . . . for your sake."

"It isn't," I assured her.

"Is Chase that blond guy by the truck?" Allison asked as we walked out the security gates and onto the street.

I nodded, noticing that Chase was tilting his head and staring down the street with deep concentration. Who or what was he listening to? I wondered.

"Hmmm . . . he's a total hunk." Allison grinned. "And you say he came here to warn me? Like a real hero type?"

I nodded, feeling a swift stab of jealousy. Allison had taken off her cap and smoothed back her long shiny hair. Even in the rumpled, sloppy overalls she had an unusual beauty. Chase was sure to notice.

But when I neared the truck, Chase was still staring down the street, not paying attention to either Allison or me. When he turned toward us, I immediately realized something was wrong.

"This is Allison," I began. "I told her

you'd explain —"

"No time for that!" Chase interrupted. "Get in the truck!"

"Why?" I looked around for danger, and saw none.

"What's going on?" Allison's mouth dropped open. "I'm not going anywhere until you tell me —"

"I heard them! They're coming!" Chase yanked open the passenger door and pushed me inside. Then he grabbed Allison's arm. "Move it, *now!* We have to leave!"

"But —" Allison sounded more confused than frightened.

"Don't waste time with questions! Dr. Victor and Geneva are almost here!" Chase pointed down the street and I saw a white car about a block away. "Now get in the truck or we're all dead!"

EIGHTEEN

"Am I being kidnapped?" Allison asked as the truck roared away from the curb and burned rubber down the road.

"You're being rescued," I replied, turning to look out the window. "Chase! They're following us!"

"I know." His jaw was clenched and he leaned closer to the wheel. "Fasten your seat belts. I'll try to lose them."

"Them? Who?" Allison shrieked, holding on to my shoulder as the car swerved around a corner.

"Bad guys," I said. "And they're still after us!"

"I know," Chase replied grimly.

"So lose them already!" I tensed when we made another sharp turn onto a hilly street that seemed to shoot straight up to the sky. As the truck neared the top, its engine chugged and rattled, slowing rather than increasing speed. "Hurry, Chase!"

"I'm trying! Just sit back and let me drive!"

The truck crested the hill and I held my breath as we drove faster and faster — like jumping off a cliff, only we were on four wheels that seemed to spin at warp speed.

"I can't believe that white car is really after us!" Allison turned her head to stare out the rear window. "This is so cool. Like something out of a movie!"

"It's not a movie." I dug my fingers into the seat to hold on for dear life. "And it's definitely not cool."

"You're really scared, aren't you?" Allison's dark eyes widened. "But why? Are the people in the white car gonna start shooting?"

"I hope not," Chase said, turning the wheel sharply to the right, onto a one-way street — but going the *wrong* way.

"We're gonna crash!"

"Not if I can help it. Hang tight!" Chase swerved again, cars honking and tires squealing, but at least now we were going in the right direction.

Allison grabbed my arm when she was thrown against me and I cried out in pain. "Sorry," she said quickly, letting go and frowning at the dark red marks on my arm. "I didn't mean to squeeze so hard. But what's going on here? Why are those people chasing us?"

"They think I'm a clone and . . ." We swerved around a truck, braking suddenly when an old woman pushing a cart stepped onto the road. "And they want you and Chase because you *are* clones!"

"A clone?" Allison's disbelief was evident. "Me?"

Chase was focused on driving, his gaze both in the rearview mirror and on the road, so I knew it was up to me to fill Allison in. "Are you adopted?" I asked her.

"No."

"No?" I repeated, then shrieked as Chase sped through a red light. "But your name was on the clone list and the bad guys are after you, too."

"That's crazy!"

I twisted around. "They're still behind us!" I turned back to Allison. "But you have to be adopted!"

"Not according to my parents. So either your list is wrong or my parents have lied to me my whole life." Allison's hands flew up as the car sailed over a bump. "And I'm betting on my parents lying."

"Why?" Chase asked.

"Being adopted would explain so much . . . hey, look out!"

Chase braked quick to avoid a woman pushing a stroller, then jerked to the right, climbing on the sidewalk and knocking over a sign that advertised a large pizza for seven dollars.

Looking behind my shoulder, I saw the white car dodge oncoming traffic, but keep on going. They were still behind us. My heart sped up as I made out two figures in the front seat, a woman driver and a man passenger.

"I've always been so different from my parents," Allison was saying, sounding amazingly calm.

"How different?" Chase asked, turning again and ascending up yet another steep hill.

"Father is like this big honcho in politics and Mother plays the perfect politician's wife, following the daily schedule Father's secretary gives her."

"But your parents must care about you."

"Oh, do they?" Allison said doubtfully. "They only care about appearances. That's why they shipped me off to Princess Prison, the 'right' place for a councilman's daughter."

"*Yeeees!*" Chase suddenly shouted, pumping his fist in the air for victory. "They just got trapped behind a truck at a red light!"

"Great!" I exclaimed.

"Way to go, Chase," Allison said with a smile. "And as far as I'm concerned, you can just keep on driving far away from my dumb school. I'm sick of that place!"

"It did look like a prison," I admitted.

"It's worse." Allison made a face. "I can recite where each fork and spoon should be on the table and I know exactly how to hold my graceful little pinky when sipping tea. But I'd rather work with lumber and nails, maybe go through a carpenter's apprentice program."

"Carpentry's cool. . . . Damn! They're behind us again!" Chase braked sharply to avoid a slow-moving station wagon, then zipped into the next lane, sliced through a parking lot, and made a sharp left.

I held on to Allison and the seat, fighting to stay upright.

"My parents don't want me to be a carpenter," Allison continued. She hit her palm on her paint-splattered pants and pursed her lips defiantly. "But they can't stop me forever."

"Where are we going anyway?" I asked Chase.

"Don't know. Just away from them. Another few turns and they're in my dust. Hold on!"

"I'm holding!" I cried, then glanced over

129

to Allison. "At least when you're eighteen, you can do what you want."

"Or sooner . . ." An odd gleam came to her brown eyes. "If I find out something scandalous about my family, I could use it to my advantage. Your clone story has me thinking. There's a secret I've never told anyone."

"What?" I saw stopped traffic up ahead and looked nervously at Chase. His mouth twisted in determination, and suddenly he spun the truck around in a U-turn, cutting in front of a large bus, tires squealing and horns honking.

"Now let them try to follow us!" Chase declared with a grin.

"Wow! Way to go, Chase! You lost them!" Allison laughed.

"For now, anyway."

"You were great!" Allison raved. "This is the most excitement I've had in a long time!"

"Too much excitement for me," I admitted, then wished I could take back my words when I noticed the admiring glance Chase gave Allison. Not only was Allison gorgeous, but she seemed fearless.

We turned onto a side street which dipped down and then up again like a roller coaster. These San Francisco streets were crazy!

Chase was frowning and I asked him why.

He pointed to the gas gauge. It was leaning heavily on the red Empty mark. "We have to get some gas. Shout out when you see a station."

Right away, Allison pointed to the left. "There's one."

"Great!" Chase slowed into the turning lane and glanced at Allison. "You were going to tell us some secret. What?"

"Oh, my secret?" She frowned. "A few years ago I overheard my mother talking to her doctor on the phone and she said the oddest thing."

"What?" Chase asked Allison as he pulled into the gas station.

"That she'd never been able to have children."

"But she'd had you," I pointed out.

"That's why it was so odd. When I confronted her, she explained that she couldn't have any more children *after* she'd had me. Only I knew she was lying. She was twisting her pearls like she always does when she lies. And I started noticing how different my parents and I were. Oh, Mom and I both have blond hair and brown eyes, so people say we look alike. But our faces and hands are shaped differently. I'm not like Father, either."

Chase gave her a sideways look. "So you could be adopted?"

"Maybe." She shrugged. "But for my parents to keep it a secret, there has to be more. Like maybe I was illegally adopted. I never thought I could be some kind of science experiment, but stranger things have happened. I've watched that TV show, *Weird and Weirder*, so if Elvis is alive and aliens are running our government, anything is possible."

Elvis? Aliens? Hmmm.

"So after you fill up, where are we headed?" Allison asked. "The police?"

"No way," Chase said roughly. "They'd never believe us. Dr. Victor is respected and wealthy. We have to hide."

"But where?" I worried, thinking of my uncle and how he'd been attacked in our home. "Dr. Victor and Geneva keep finding us. At my house, in the hospital, and now in San Francisco."

Chase didn't answer, but his silence told me he didn't have any answers. He parked at a pump, stepped out of the truck, and began to pump gas. I kept my eyes on the road, watchful for our pursuers. But we seemed to have lost them.

I hoped.

"I still can't believe all of this," Allison

marveled. "A car chase and bad guys after us because they think we're clones."

"You and Chase are the clones. Not me. My uncle Jim was one of the doctors on the clone experiment. My parents died in a train wreck, so Uncle Jim took me in. When he got hurt, he gave me the list of clones' names and asked me to warn you, Chase, and at least two others."

"Others?" Allison's face lit up. "Ooh! I want to meet them. Where are they? Do any of them look like me?"

"If they're lucky," Chase teased.

I felt a sharp stab of jealousy, and steered the conversation back on track. "We don't know much about them. Eric lives at Route 3, Box 77, in Marshall, Texas, and Sandee is at 1300 Mathes Place, Apartment #339, Denver, Colorado."

"You memorized their addresses?"

"Not on purpose. I just naturally remember stuff like that." I shrugged. "There's also another girl clone, but the list was torn so we don't have her address. When my uncle gets better, he can clue us in."

"What will we do until then?"

"I have no idea. But we can't let Dr. Victor and Geneva find us. They're killers." I trembled. "And who knows how many other people might be involved. They could have hired someone to watch the hospital, my house, or your school."

"You can't be serious," Allison said skeptically.

"Dead serious. They're one step ahead of us and there are so many things we still don't know. Like why the doctors secretly created clones in the first place, what went wrong, and why Chase has this way-cool hearing. You know, he can hear through walls and long distances away."

"He can?" Allison asked. "Wow! Wish I had hearing like that!"

"Don't you?"

"No. Although there is something cool I can do —"

"What?"

"Maybe I'll show you later." Allison gave me a mischievous look. "Here comes Chase."

As Chase climbed back into the car, he looked tired and discouraged. "The good news is we have a full tank. The bad news is I'm almost out of cash. I have a credit card, but it won't go far, either."

"So what's the problem?" Allison genuinely looked puzzled.

"We're in real trouble here, Allison," Chase said impatiently. "You can't go back to your school any more than I can return to Reno or Varina can go to Liberty Hills. But it'll take money to hide."

"Don't forget Eric and Sandee," I added as the car slowly left the gas station. "We need to warn them."

"If we ever get out of San Francisco." Chase shook his head in exasperation. He quickly spun the wheel around, receiving angry honks and hand gestures. "How in the world are we going to get all the way to Texas and Colorado?"

"We can fly," Allison suggested.

"That would cost way too much," I said.

"Money is not a problem. I have plenty of cash and credit cards. Although not on me." Allison groaned. "My purse is back at school."

"And we can't go there," I pointed out. "That's the first place Dr. Victor and Geneva will look. They might be there right now searching for us."

"But they won't find us if we're careful." Allison arched her dark blond brows. "Besides, I can't just take off without some kind of story or my teachers will phone my parents or the cops."

I shook my head. "It's not safe to go back."

"Varina's right." Chase's gaze darted back and forth, on the lookout for trouble. "We can't risk it."

"But we have to," Allison insisted with a determined expression. "I know we're in danger. Maybe I'm even a clone. I'm believing you, so the least you can do is trust me. Which means going back to my school. It's our only chance."

NINETEEN

I folded my arms against my chest, staring straight ahead, too angry to look at either Chase or Allison. How could Chase be lame enough to give in to Allison? Sure, Allison's credit cards and cash would help, but not if it meant being captured, or worse. I shuddered, unable to get Geneva's syringe out of my mind. I was scared, but even more, I was hurt because Chase had sided with Allison against me.

Ignoring my arguments, Chase headed back to the Pacific Palace for Young Ladies.

"Don't be mad, Varina," Allison pleaded. "I promise to hurry. And I know a side road we can park on where no one will see us. Really, we'll be perfectly safe."

There was no such thing as safe. Chase's parents and my uncle were proof of that grim fact. So I didn't answer.

Instead of parking in front of the building, Allison directed Chase to a quiet side street where tall trees and lush bushes shaded the truck. When she scooted out of the truck, I didn't wave good-bye, although in my head I whispered a fervent "Good luck."

Then Allison used a side entrance to sneak into her school.

"Waiting makes me uneasy," Chase admitted, tapping his fingers on the steering wheel.

"Me, too." I reclined my seat. "I'll be glad when this is all over."

"Yeah. If we get that lucky."

"I wish I could just sleep and wake up to find this all a bad dream." I yawned, fatigue suddenly making my eyes water and my head ache. How long had it been since I slept? Not since I'd passed out from the drugged soda right before Chase came to help me get away. No wonder I was anxious and exhausted. So much had happened in such a short time. Meeting Chase, the break-in and attack on my uncle, and then the appearance of Geneva. And to think that just two days ago my biggest worry had been going to a new school with an ugly zit on my face.

Now I was worrying about life and death.

My eyes closed, which felt *so* good. My thoughts floated away and images swarmed like a funnel in my mind — Geneva smiling malevolently, my uncle lying helplessly in a hospital bed, Chase running as he looked over his shoulder. Fear. I could feel his stark fear. Would he ever be able to stop running?

Then peace surrounded me and there was the angel-woman. Only this time she was with someone, a young Uncle Jim.

"We should give her a real name," the man told the angel-woman. "Not a number like the others."

"I call her Little Princess."

"She deserves her own unique name. She's going to be smart and beautiful like you."

"She'll be better than me." The angel-woman laughed softly. "I made sure of that."

Then the image grew cloudy and there were no more words, only a sense of warmth, love, and protection.

"Varina! Wake up!"

Rough fingers dug into my shoulder and I heard my name again. "W-What?" I blinked.

"We've got company," Chase said in a harsh whisper.

"Is Allison back?"

"Not yet." His gray-blue eyes flashed as if he was readying for a fight. "But look over there — in front of the building."

I lifted my head and followed his gaze. A pale white Buick was parked by the gates of the Pacific Palace.

"Oh, no! They've found us!"

"Not yet," Chase assured. "They don't know we're here. But they're looking . . ."

I scooted down in my seat, peeking out the truck window. "Geneva's getting out of her car."

"Dr. Victor is there, too," Chase said with a murderous twist of his mouth. "And a woman just opened the gate, inviting them inside."

"Inside?" I gulped. "But Allison is still in there! She'll be trapped!"

TWENTY

"We have to rescue Allison!" I said, opening the car door, ready to storm the building.

"Wait." Chase pulled me back. "Allison's okay."

I recognized the way he held his head tilted to one side, and realized he was listening.

Would I ever get used to his incredible hearing?

"You sure?"

"They haven't found her . . . not yet."

"What's happening in there?"

"I'm zooming in on Geneva and Dr. Victor. Gotta concentrate so I can block out other conversations. Okay, I found them. Geneva is saying, 'How kind of you to allow us a visit on such . . . short notice, Mrs. Vaughn. Allison's parents . . . asked us to check on the dear girl . . . while we were visiting your lovely city.' "

"Lies," I grumbled.

"Mrs. Vaughn is talking now, saying she

141

hopes they have time for a bay cruise or a visit to the botanical gardens while in San Francisco. Blah, blah, blah. Nothing interesting yet . . . Oh, now something's happening! Dr. Victor asked where Allison is. And Mrs. Vaughn called someone named Reanna to go get her."

"I hope Allison is hiding. Can you hear her?"

"No. There's a lot of talking in that building and I have to concentrate to hear only one conversation. But Dr. Victor is talking —" Chase stared intently into space, his mouth pursed tightly and his eyes narrowed with fury. His hatred of Dr. Victor was real and dangerous.

"What's going on?" I hesitated, then touched Chase's arm to get his notice. "Where's Allison?"

Chase shook his head and gestured for me to be quiet.

I watched and waited for him to tell me more, occasionally looking out the window, hoping to see Allison. But nothing.

Finally, Chase turned to me with a sigh of relief. "That girl, Reanna, came back. She can't find Allison."

"Whew!" I gave a low whistle. "Way to go, Allison!"

"And there's more!" Chase paused, his

gray-blue eyes lighting up. "There was a note on Allison's bed, saying she was spending the night with her cousin Miriam."

"Think she really has a cousin Miriam?"

"Who cares? She made it out of there. That's what matters."

"Good! And leaving a note was a smart move."

"But where is she now?" Chase worried.

"There!" I cried suddenly, recognizing the slim figure who hurried toward us, her long hair buried in a sports cap. She had switched from sloppy coveralls to a loose denim jumper and a pale yellow T-shirt. When she burst inside the car, her cheeks were flushed with excitement and she wore a triumphant smile.

"Mission accomplished!" Allison rejoiced, reaching for her seat belt. "Wow! Close call! I only *just* barely got away. Those bad dudes were asking about me."

"Chase heard them talking to Mrs. Vaughn."

"She's the headmistress." Allison raised her blond brows curiously. "But how'd Chase hear . . . oh, yeah, Mr. Super Ears."

"Don't joke about it," Chase warned.

"Or what?" she teased. "Remember, you need me . . . or at least my money."

"She's got you there." I glanced around,

anxious to get out of there. "We'd better hurry. They'll be after us again."

"Not if I slow them down first," Chase said with a wicked expression. He pulled out a multiuse knife from his pocket and popped open a slim silver blade. "A few slashes in their tires and they won't be able to do anything for a while."

"What is it with guys and weapons?" Allison rolled her eyes. "Besides, tires can be replaced."

"So you have a better idea?" he retorted.

"Absolutely! You aren't the only one with hidden talents. Just watch me!" She laughed, then burst out of the car before we could question her.

What in the world was Allison planning? I watched as she crept around the wrought-iron fence, staying low and in the shadows of manicured shrubbery. Beside me, I saw the scowl on Chase's face and sensed his irritation.

"We don't have time for games," he muttered.

"That's for sure. I knew coming here was too risky." I wrung my hands on my lap, glancing at my watch as minutes ticked away. "We have to get away before it's too late."

Chase tilted his head, zooming in on some distant voices that I could only imagine.

"Dr. Victor and Geneva are still inside, but they're saying good-bye to Mrs. Vaughn."

"Allison had better hurry. She's going to get us all killed. She acted like she had a plan, but what can she possibly do?" I stared off in the distance, watching Allison as she reached Geneva's white Buick. She walked to the driver's door, grabbed the handle, then pulled the door open. "What's she doing?"

"No clue here." Chase shook his head, glancing around, tense with alertness. "I should have stopped her. Dr. Victor and Geneva are leaving now!"

"Oh, no!" I said, more anxious by the minute. In one direction I could see the stained-glass double doors opening and two distant figures leaving the school. And in the other direction, there was Allison, reaching inside Geneva's car with both hands. . . .

"I'm seeing things!" I cried. "I mean, I have to be because what Allison just did is impossible!"

"But she did it!" Chase's jaw nearly dropped to the floor and his eyes were wide with astonishment. "Wow! You know what this means?"

I just shook my head, totally amazed and awed.

"It means that Allison has a special power, too!"

Twenty-One

When Allison returned to the car seconds later, breathless and triumphant, she showed off her incredible trophy: a large white leather-covered steering wheel.

"Ta da! Drumroll, please!" she rang out, tossing the round wheel behind the seat. "Let's see those bad dudes drive off without their steering wheel!"

"But-But how?" I stammered.

"I simply took it." Her dark eyes twinkled with mischievous delight. "Easy as picking up a piece of paper. Oh, didn't I mention that I'm very strong? *Unusually strong.*"

"You pulled the wheel off?" Chase asked with a shake of his blond head as he reached forward and turned on the engine.

"Yeah. No biggie. I can also carry heavy cement blocks, throw balls so high they vanish in the sky, and straighten crooked nails — which really comes in handy." Allison chuckled. "Let's put some miles between us and that creepy couple."

"But where can we go?" I asked.

"The airport," Allison said. "Now that I have my credit cards, we can travel anywhere. London, Paris, Australia. But I vote for finding the other clones you mentioned."

"Eric in Texas or Sandee in Colorado?" I asked.

"Whichever flight leaves ASAP," Allison answered.

I stared at her, studying the tight muscles in her slender arms and wondering how a cloning experiment created her super strength as well as Chase's incredible hearing. Did my uncle know about these amazing skills? If so, how could he spend years grading papers and being involved in routine research when he could have been improving DNA and making fantastic scientific breakthroughs? What a waste! Or maybe he didn't know. Yeah, that had to be it. The doctors must have ended the cloning experiment too soon. Chase said his hearing had improved with age, so it's possible that none of the doctors realized the clones they created were so incredible.

Chase drove away from the Victorian houses, away from Geneva and Dr. Victor, and his grip on the wheel relaxed.

"I can't believe your strength," Chase told

Allison. "No way I could rip a steering wheel off like that."

"Cool, huh? And it feels so great to finally tell someone."

"You've never told anyone?" I asked, my legs cramped as I resumed the middle "pretzel" position.

"No one." She tightened the cap on her head, tucking in loose dark blond tendrils. "If my father ever found out, he'd think I was crazy and ship me off to a psychiatric institute. No thanks! So I've only tried out my strength when I was alone."

"How long have you had it?" Chase asked.

"About two years. Lately I've gotten even stronger." She rolled down her window, letting in moist, salty air. "At first I was afraid I *was* crazy, but after a while I relaxed and had fun."

"I know what you mean," Chase said with a nod, flipping on his right turning signal and veering onto a freeway ramp. "I found out about my hearing when I was around thirteen."

"Puberty," I said, finding some logic in this very illogical situation. "You two probably had the powers all along, but they didn't' show up till you were older."

"Like growing a beard." Chase touched

his stubbly chin.

"Or getting tall . . . taller than my own father," Allison complained.

They went on to compare their "powerful" experiences, and I listened quietly. Sitting between them, I was like a third arm, foot, or eyeball; useful but out of place. They had so much in common, and I couldn't help but feel left out. Even worse, with gorgeous Allison flexing her super muscles for Chase, he'd probably never notice me now. Allison and Chase were the perfect pair. I was simply extra baggage.

Okay, so my resentment was childish, and I knew it. Being moody was probably my worst fault. I'd always been moody. One minute I'd be flying high with joy and then *bam!* someone would say something sharp or I'd make a mistake, and then sink into sadness. To avoid this, I tried to keep my life calm and uncomplicated, so I wouldn't have to cope with my swirling emotions.

Unfortunately, my life had been anything but calm lately.

And even though I knew logically that Dr. Victor and Geneva couldn't follow us without a steering wheel, I couldn't relax. I kept looking out the windows, jumping whenever I saw a white car. Maybe they had a different car now. We could rocket to the moon, and they'd probably still come after us.

Chase and Allison seemed more relaxed when we arrived at the airport, but I continued to worry. And I insisted we park the car in the farthest lot, hidden between a camper and a big rig.

Okay, I was getting paranoid. But the more cautious we were, the better chance we'd have for survival.

Allison took charge, standing poised and confident as she made three reservations for a flight to Texas. I wanted to use fake names, but with airport security so tight, that was out of the question. Chase had to show his driver's license, and Allison and I showed our school ID cards. I only hoped we weren't leaving a trail that Dr. Victor and Geneva could follow.

And then one hour later, we were high in the air, winging our way to Texas.

Eric Prince, clone number three, here we come!

TWENTY-TWO

Getting to the town of Marshall took longer than we'd expected. The only flight available flew into Dallas — over a hundred miles from Marshall. After Chase used his own credit card to rent a car at the airport, we drove off.

We had plenty of time for talking and planning. We each had different ideas and couldn't agree on a course of action. Allison preferred a direct approach — striding into Eric's home and physically taking him away so he'd be safe. Chase argued that Eric would need to be convinced, which meant caution and tact. I agreed with Chase, and was pleased when he flashed me a grateful smile.

Still, I was afraid if we were too cautious we would waste valuable time and Dr. Victor and Geneva might catch up to us. If Dr. Victor could set a fire that killed two innocent people, who knew what other horrors he was capable of.

And I remembered the look on Chase's

face when we'd been in the hospital and he'd overheard Dr. Victor and Geneva plotting some kind of horrible testing for me — because they thought I was a clone, too. I'd had biology in school and dissected a tiny squid that had been pickled in formaldehyde. Gross. But I'd blocked out my disgust and tackled the lab work anyway. Tiny muscles, tentacles, and veins became simply a school assignment; the squid a specimen, not a living creature.

And that's exactly how I feared Dr. Victor and Geneva viewed the clones. Specimens. Experiments. Not one ounce of humanity.

"Welcome to Marshall," Chase announced. "Now we need to find out where Eric lives."

"There's a convenience store," I said, pointing out the window. "Let's stop there, get something to eat and drink, then ask for directions."

"The snacks are on me," Allison offered.

"Don't bother." I shook my head, my pride taking over. "I have some money still. Thanks, anyway."

Then we parked and entered the store. The clerk, a girl who popped pink bubble gum and flipped her long flowing cinnamon-brown hair behind her shoulders, gave us an interested look. A customer she'd been waiting on paused to stare, too. Was the caption "Teens on the Run" blazed on our foreheads, or was this just a quiet town that didn't get many outsiders? Either way, I felt an immediate wariness.

"You just passing through?" The customer, a middle-aged man with a dark gray mustache, rubbed his chin as he studied us.

"Looking for a friend," Chase answered cautiously.

"What a lovely town." Allison stepped forward, her smile as inviting as one of their own Texas beauty queens. "Good afternoon. Maybe you can help us find our friend. He lives somewhere around here."

"Be glad to," the man replied with a friendly nod. "Afternoon to you, too. What's your friend's address?"

"Route 3, Box 77," I recited, which caused Chase to give me an impressed look.

"Need more than that." The man shook his head. "Can't find folks without a street name."

"Darn," I heard Allison mutter.

"My friend's name is Eric Prince," Chase said.

"Is that right?" Immediately the man flashed a toothy grin. "Well, why didn't ya'll say so in the first place? That's only just down the road. Everyone around here knows the

Prince family. Fine folks. And if you're a friend of theirs, then you're okay by me, too."

A short time later, Chase had the directions — not the kind of directions I was used to, with street names, but inventive descriptions of turns you made at the wheat field with the lightning-split pine tree or a sharp left where the paved road ended and turned to an oil dirt road.

Chase simply smiled and thanked the man while he wrote the instructions down. Miss Congeniality Allison made small, friendly talk, clearly at ease in any social situation. Chase watched her with an amused smile. But I hung back, my resentment of Allison growing. I liked her, but with her around I felt like I was invisible.

It was only about twenty miles to the Prince home, but the drive seemed longer. They lived on the edge of nowhere, somewhere before you ran into oblivion. It was a huge relief, after miles and miles of dense woods, to see an oasis of a rambling ranch-style house with several outbuildings and spacious pasture.

Dust stirred around the truck as we drove down the long curved road to the house. As we drew closer, I noticed the busy activity of a basketball game being played on a large paved area. An orange ball flew up high, soaring toward a net, hitting the backboard, and then bouncing back into eager hands. But it wasn't the ball that seized my attention, it was the players. They didn't jump on two legs, but rolled on four wheels. The four kids who played were all in wheelchairs.

Not that this slowed them down. They tilted, whirled, and zoomed at amazing speeds, dodging each other, hands grasping for the ball, tossing to team partners, until a freckled boy propelled the ball high toward the net, right on target.

The car had slowed to a stop, and besides me I noticed the awed yet uneasy expressions on Chase's and Allison's faces. And I knew they were wondering the same thing I was.

Instead of the cloning experiment giving Eric a super trait, had it backfired and taken some ability away, leaving him with a permanent disability?

I studied the four kids playing, three boys and one girl. Was one of the boys Eric Prince? They were all mixed nationalities, sizes, and ages. Only two of the boys looked about the right age: the freckled sandy-haired boy who'd made the basket and a skinny African-American boy whose face was swallowed up by thick glasses.

Other sounds caught my attention, and I turned toward the largest building, where several people were coming outside. A few adults and even more kids. Another three girls and two boys, from kindergarten-age to teens.

Was this a school?

"Let's go find Eric," Allison declared. "Once he knows the truth, he'll come away with us."

"He won't believe us at first," Chase said.

"So I'll toss him high like a basketball and you can eavesdrop a mile away. Then he'll know we're telling the truth. Besides, he probably has some kind of super skill of his own," Allison said, her voice rising with excitement. "I wonder what it is. Hearing, strength, or something else?"

Chase nodded. "It'll be cool to find out."

I frowned, wishing I could impress Chase with an unusual skill. But my hearing and strength were only average. And Chase wasn't the type of guy to fall for an average girl.

"How should we proceed?" Chase asked, suddenly turning to me with a half smile that made my heart jump. "Any ideas, Varina?"

"Let's ask for Eric," I said quietly. "Then see what happens."

"And if they ask how we know Eric, we

can pretend to be talent scouts or those people who give away prize money." Allison's dark eyes danced with mischief.

"I'll just say my uncle knew Eric when he was little and asked us to look him up. It's safer to stick to the truth."

"Dull, but makes sense." Allison pursued her lips in disappointment. "That'll work, too."

"So get moving already." Chase pocketed his car keys and opened the door. "Come on, let's go find Eric."

Allison stepped out, and I followed. A small group of people, and even a few dogs with their tails wagging, came over to greet us. I counted over a dozen kids, mostly in wheelchairs, although a few had leg braces. I guessed this must be a special school, and the two adults, a middle-aged man and woman, were probably teachers.

"Afternoon." The woman stepped forward with her hand extended and friendly smile on her round, tanned face. "I'm Melody Ann Prince and this is my husband, Larry."

"Nice to meet you." Chase held out his hand, slipping into the role of spokesman for our trio. He cleared his throat. "I'm Chase Rinaldi, and these are my friends, Allison Beaumont and Varina Fergus."

I smiled. "Hi."

"Hello!" Allison seemed to sparkle. "What a lovely school you have."

"Oh my, this isn't a school. It's our home." Mrs. Prince tucked back a light brown curl and chuckled. "And these are our children."

"All of them?" I asked, astonished.

"Ten to be exact, six boys and four girls. Adopted, of course." Mrs. Prince laughed. "Larry and I have lived here since our eldest, Larry Joe, was in diapers and now our youngest, Michele May, is three. Time sure does just whip away when you're raising a family."

"It sure does at that," Larry said with a nod that tipped his dusty western hat forward. "What brings you folks way out here? Is there something we can do for ya'll?"

Chase looked at me, I looked at Allison, who in turn looked back at me. Okay, I could handle this. As long as I didn't scare these nice people by mentioning the "C" word.

Stick to the truth, I reminded myself. So I explained that my uncle, who was in the hospital, had given me a piece of paper with some names and addresses, asking me to find these people.

"That's why we're here. We're looking for

Eric Prince," I added, wondering which boy was Eric.

"Your uncle knows our Eric?" Mr. Prince said, furrowing his brow. "What's your uncle's name?"

"Professor James Fergus," I answered.

Mr. Prince shrugged. "Never heard of him."

"Maybe this is about Eric *before*." Mrs. Prince's tan seemed to fade away and her hands trembled. She leaned against her husband. "Larry, we always feared someone might come . . ."

Her husband nodded grimly, then turned away from us and called to the group of kids who had been playing basketball. "Eric! Get over here."

So Eric *was* one of the wheelchair athletes.

"Yeah, Dad!" Eric, the skinny boy with glasses, tossed the basketball to the freckled boy. Eric grinned good-naturedly and then did something so unexpected that Chase, Allison, and I let out sharp, shocked gasps.

TWENTY-THREE

Eric Prince stood up from his wheelchair and walked.

"But-But his legs work fine!" Allison exclaimed.

"Why the wheelchair?" I wanted to know.

"Because he's a great kid who loves to play basketball with his siblings," Mrs. Prince answered, her face softening as Eric came over and hugged her.

"What's up, Mom?" Eric asked, wiping his sweaty brow.

Mrs. Prince glanced at us fearfully, her chin trembling, then she clutched her hands. "Eric, these people want to talk with you."

Eric's blank eyes pooled with uncertainty. "Why?"

"We aren't sure, son," Mr. Prince spoke quietly. "But you hear them out. It's the right thing to do. And then we'll talk things over later."

Then Mr. Prince took his wife by the hand, gestured for the other kids to leave, and left Eric alone with us. I could feel the questions in Eric's mind; a pearl haze of curiosity.

"So what's this about?" Eric asked, pushing up his thick glasses. He wore a green T-shirt with the caption "Hackers Byte," and his dark black jeans were a few inches short on him, as if he'd grown recently. "Should I know you guys?"

"No," Allison answered, offering a gentle smile. "But we're very happy to find you."

"Eric, we know about your past," Chase explained. "You probably won't believe us, but we're here to help you."

"Why would I need help?" Eric's skinny face spread to a shaky grin.

"We can tell you about your birth," I said carefully.

"Really?" He frowned, his loyalty to his family and his curiosity clearly at odds. "Well . . . I don't want to know. Mom and Dad are great and I wouldn't do anything to hurt them. Besides, my biological parents just dumped me off when I was a baby —"

"A year and a half old," Chase said. "Only that's not who left you."

I bit my lower lip. "It was my uncle."

"*What?*" Eric exclaimed.

Between Chase, Allison, and I, we managed to get the whole weird story out. Of course, Eric was doubtful. He claimed cloning was something out of science-fiction novels, not his own life. But when Allison showed off by lifting Chase over her head as if he were a weightless balloon, Eric regarded us with new respect.

"Wow! Like a role I'd play with my computer games — only *real* not virutal. You really do have super powers!"

"Chase has power, too," Allison added. "He can hear through walls and across distances."

"Way cool! But what about her?" Eric pointed to me. "What kind of super power does she have?"

"None." I smiled, deciding that it was good being just an ordinary girl. While I envied the way Allison dazzled Chase with her strength, I was glad I didn't have to deal with the whole clone thing. The powers were interesting, and I might enjoy studying cloning from a scientific angle, but it was hard enough to fit in with other kids without being a sci-fi experiment.

"Varina's uncle was one of the doctors who secretly created clones," Chase told Eric.

"And you really think I'm a clone?" Eric's eyes magnified behind his thick glasses. "So, like, my eyes are my super power?"

"Your eyes?" Allison asked doubtfully. "Maybe you didn't understand. My strength is mega-powerful, and so is Chase's hearing —"

"But so are my eyes!" Eric exclaimed.

"You wear glasses. Very thick glasses," I pointed out, wondering if Eric was a bit simpleminded. "You wouldn't need glasses at all if you had an extra power."

"You don't get it." Eric lifted his glasses, slipped them into his pocket, then blinked rapidly. He wobbled and leaned to one side then the other, as if he had lost his balance.

"You okay?" Chase reached out to steady him.

"Yeah, but without the glasses I get dizzy." Eric rubbed his eyes. "I'm farsighted in a major way, although I don't usually talk about it."

"What do you mean?" Chase's dark brows puckered together.

"If I take off my glasses, I can see far away. Like I can see that squirrel carrying a nut up in that oak tree past the barn."

I looked toward the barn, but I couldn't even see the oak tree he was talking about much less a squirrel and a tiny nut!

"My far-off sight is confusing," Eric added. "Without my glasses, I fall down or bump into things. Kids at school think I'm a klutz, but I don't mind. I'm not gonna brag about having super eyesight."

"When did this start?" Chase asked.

"About two years ago."

Allison, Chase and I shared a deep look. This was beginning to make sense; another puzzle piece fitting into place. And I felt a heady sense of relief. Allison and Eric had been found and they were okay. Now all we had to do was find Sandee, and then we could return home, to the hospital, where hopefully my uncle would be well enough to offer a safe solution.

And my life could resume. I'd go back to school, somehow convince Starr to give me another chance, earn good grades, join some cool clubs, and maybe get to know Chase better. It would be so great. And I'd try to be more open to friends, not so shut off. A totally typical sixteen year old: me.

I was imagining the slinky emerald-green formal I'd wear to my first prom and how great Chase would look in a tux, when I realized we were headed toward the main house. Eric was convinced and he seemed okay with his newfound history. But he wanted to share everything with his family.

"We don't keep secrets around here," Eric said with a firm set of his jaw.

"But you're in danger, Eric," Chase insisted. "Dr. Victor killed my parents. You don't want to put your family in danger, do you?"

"That's their choice. Either you come with me while I explain or just leave. You can trust my parents. They're the greatest."

Chase scowled, then glanced away, and for that moment I felt the grief he usually managed to hide. I could only imagine how heartbroken I'd be if Uncle Jim didn't survive. Totally devastated, as Chase surely was. And I wished I could put my arms around him to comfort him, only I didn't dare.

And we couldn't change Eric's mind, either. Which is why a short time later, Eric's parents were listening to our story with concerned astonishment. Chase had clammed up, so Allison and I did the explaining. Naturally, they didn't believe us.

"But my eyesight is proof!" Eric insisted, which caused his mother to put her finger to her lips and shush him.

"Don't talk about being different," Mrs. Prince warned.

"He's not the only one who's different." Allison stood up, walked over to the refrigerator, and lifted it up with ease.

Mrs. and Mr. Prince gasped, but after that it was easier to convince them. And when we finished the whole story, there were no more doubts.

Mrs. Prince wrapped her arms around Eric. "It doesn't matter who brought you into this world," she told him softly, "I'm grateful to them."

"You're our son," Mr. Prince added gruffly. "That's all. Nothing else matters. And we'll make sure you're safe."

"He'd be safer with us," Allison said.

"Only if you stay here with us," Mrs. Prince replied with a faint smile. "You children are welcome here. There's always room for a few more."

I felt a warm wash of emotion at her kindness. What a wonderful mother . . . probably as wonderful as my own mother had been.

Still, we could not stay here. Sandee Yoon was out there, unprotected and defenseless. Besides, if we stood still for too long, Dr. Victor and Geneva might find us.

Unfortunately, there was no convincing Eric of the real danger. He was stubborn and totally refused to come with us.

Disappointed, we walked back to the truck. Eric led the way, patting a golden retriever named Taffy and a yellow lab pup named Renegade who bounded beside him.

"Sorry it turned out like this," Eric said.

"Can't blame you for staying," Chase admitted, his voice gruff. "Just watch your back, pal."

"No worry there. My whole family will be watching out for me — practically an army of support."

"Lucky you," Allison said with a smile. "But we're kind of like family now, too. Not exactly brothers and sisters, more like cousins. And we clone cousins need to stick together."

Chase and Eric chuckled; I just shrugged. Somehow it felt like we'd failed. And I hated to let my uncle down. I just hoped he was okay. I'd go back to him. Soon.

"But you know something kind of odd," Eric was saying. "I'd forgotten about it, but maybe it has to do with being a clone."

"What?" Chase asked with raised brows.

Eric bent down and rolled down one of his socks. Then he pointed at a dark spot on his ankle. "This here tattoo. It's not much bigger than my thumbnail, so I never put my thought to it. But maybe you guys know something about those numbers? It says 229B."

"Wow!" Chase exclaimed. "I have one just like that!"

"Really?" Eric asked in surprise.

"Yeah. Only mine says 611B!"

"Totally amazing," Allison said, shaking

her dark blond head with wonder.

The boys turned to look at her, but I just stood there, too stunned to move or speak.

"What about you, Allison?" Chase asked eagerly. "Do you have numbers tattooed on your ankle?"

"There's a scar there, but no numbers," Allison admitted with puzzlement. "If there ever was a tattoo, I don't have it now."

"But . . ." I tried to speak, a roar swelling in my head.

They turned to me and Chase asked, "What Varina?"

"But I —" My body trembled as I choked out, "I-I do . . . I can't, and yet I do. . . . I-I have a tattoo."

Twenty-Four

I'd never felt so strange before, overwhelmed by powerful emotions that changed my view of the world. Chase, Allison, and Eric were standing beside me and yet their images swirled in dizzy rainbow hues as my mind whirled.

I couldn't have a tattoo.

Not possible . . . because that would make me a clone.

And no way could that be true.

Chase, Allison, Eric, and Sandee were clones. Not me. Not ever. No way. . . . Please . . .

And suddenly voices and images swirled in my head. The blue ocean, a white and chrome room, and the sound of crying. Babies crying.

"Can't you shut them up?" a man snarled. I was small, sitting on a pale pink blanket, and this man scared me. His shiny dark head shined yellow from the bright overhead light, and I realized who he was. Dr.

Mansfield Victor.

Another voice interrupted. A little blond boy scowled at Dr. Victor. "They're only crying 'cause you scared them," the boy accused.

"Go back to your room," Dr. Victor ordered. "My work here doesn't concern you."

"I'm gonna tell Dr. Hart!" the boy retorted. "You're mean and I hate you."

"Is that so?" Dr. Victor narrowed his dark eyes. "Do you hate me enough to kill me?" Then he began to laugh.

The laughter rang in my ears and the images faded. I realized I was standing outside, with my hands on the sides of my head, tears streaming down my face.

"Varina!" Allison cried. "What's wrong?"

"Are you okay?" Chase asked gently, putting his arms around me and holding me tight, which should have been wonderful, only I was too upset. I wanted to rage against a truth I could no longer deny.

Chase had been the blond boy in my memory. And I'd been there on the yacht with him. I'd smelled the ocean, felt the soft baby blanket beneath me, and heard the angry voice of Dr. Victor. I wasn't an ordinary girl and I'd probably never wear a slinky emerald-green dress to a prom.

Reaching down, I pulled up the bottom hem of my jeans, rolled back my white cotton sock, and pointed numbly to the tattoo: 1025G. The mark of a clone.

"It's real," I sobbed, turning to find Allison and seeing caring and concern in her eyes.

"It's not so bad, Varina," Allison soothed, lightly patting my head. "So you're a clone. Join the club."

"But I can't be!"

"Why not?" Chase asked, his face flushing darkly. "You're the one who said being a clone would be interesting. Like being a twin."

"Well, I was wrong. It's not interesting. I never asked to be an experiment!" I clenched my fists to my sides. "How could my uncle hide this from me?"

"He did it to all of us," Allison said.

"Yeah," Eric added, hanging back shyly. "At least we got some powers, too."

"Powers? But I don't have any —" I stopped, suddenly realizing how unusual it was to remember facts and conversations from years ago. Yet I'd flashed back to a time when I was just a baby. And I could memorize addresses and homework assignments. Perhaps I did have a clone skill.

"What is it, Varina?" Chase asked.

"I-I remembered you . . ." I rubbed my head. "From a long time ago. I heard Dr. Victor yelling and babies crying. I'm afraid my memory might be unusual . . . like your powers."

"A super memory?" Eric asked with wide dark eyes. "Cool!"

"But I don't want to be different."

"Obviously you are, Varina," Chase said impatiently. "So just deal with it. There's no time to freak out. We still have one more clone to find."

"Why should we?" I snapped. "Maybe Sandee's happy in her home, has lots of friends, and probably even a cool boyfriend. Why mess up her life?"

"Our lives aren't messed up." Allison's mouth pursed together with quick anger. "In fact my life has never been more thrilling."

"Face reality, Varina," Chase ordered. "If we can handle the truth, so can you."

"The truth?" I whimpered, looking down at my ankle and trying hard not to cry. 1025G. A number, not a name.

When I'd asked my uncle how I'd gotten the tattoo, he'd shrugged and said I'd always had it. "Maybe it's a birthmark," he suggested. But birthmarks were unusual shapes, not tiny numbers. And whenever anyone saw the tattoo they asked what 1025G meant, which was embarrassing. So I stopped going barefoot and I never wore sandals. And now I knew the tattoo was there because I'd been born in a laboratory.

The wedding videos and the photographs of my parents, and all the wonderful stories told by Uncle Jim about his fun-loving, warmhearted sister . . . *all lies?*

How could they be the truth if I was a particle of DNA mixed in a floating lab and then grown like a tropical flower in a fake atmosphere? I wasn't the product of two loving parents, but the result of experimental science.

Who was I really?

Allison and Chase were saying good-bye to Eric, but I didn't want to talk to anyone, so I walked over to the car and sat inside. Alone. I needed to think, figure this out. There were still so many things that didn't add up. Maybe the tattoo was just a weird coincidence. I mean, I didn't feel like a freaky experiment, only like a mixed-up girl.

This had to be a mistake.

I could not possibly be a clone.

Yet I had a tattoo . . . almost identical to the tattoos on Chase and Eric. And although I couldn't lift heavy cars or hear through walls, I'd had unusual bursts of memory.

I glanced up when Allison came into the car. "You gonna be okay?" she asked with concern.

"Not now." I shook my head and wiped the tear that strayed down my cheek. "Not ever."

"Sure you will."

"I-I can't be a clone."

"This isn't a fatal disease. It's just biology." Allison reached for the seat belt, glancing over at Chase, who had joined us. "Varina, I don't understand why you're so upset."

"Of course *you* don't!" I bit my lip, immediately ashamed for my sharp words. Allison may be rich and gorgeous, but she didn't flaunt it. Part of me knew I was being unfair, yet the other part was too upset to care about fairness. Nothing in my life was fair anymore. "I . . . I don't want to be different."

"None of us do, but it happened." Chase reached out the window to wave good-bye to Eric, then he started the truck. "And we're in this together. We'll get through it."

"Without me."

"What's that supposed to mean?" Chase demanded, stomping the gas pedal hard, causing the motor to growl and dust to kick up.

"I'm going back to California."

Allison turned to me, a puzzled look in her dark eyes. "But I thought you couldn't return. That Geneva witch was in your house and your uncle's in a coma."

"I'm still going back," I said firmly. "I have to talk to my uncle. Even if it means breaking hospital rules and staying by his bedside till he wakes up. He's the only one who can tell me the truth."

"That tattoo is truth enough." Chase's mouth set in a deep frown. "You're one of us. I suspected it, even though you fed me that line about being a year older than the others. You don't look any older than Allison or Eric."

"But I *am!* I'm turning sixteen next Saturday!"

"I doubt it," Chase said, with a glance in the rearview mirror before he merged from dirt road to paved highway.

"*Sixteen!* Not fifteen."

"Maybe your uncle lied about your age," Allison suggested.

That dizzy anger swelled in my head again, and I covered my ears. I was not going to listen to this. Being a science experiment was bad enough, but only being fifteen. . . . not sixteen! . . . that was like the worse thing in the whole world. Another whole year before I could get my driver's license.

For the rest of the drive to the airport, I clenched my mouth and didn't say another word. My mind was made up and there was no changing it. Chase and Allison could go on to Denver, chasing after poor unsuspecting Sandee Yoon, but not me.

I was going home.

TWENTY-FIVE

"You can't desert us now. We need your help to find Sandee," Chase said as my flight was being called over the loudspeakers. He took my hand, causing my heart to break a little. But I refused to be swayed.

"Since we met, all you've done is tell me what to do," I said firmly. "Now I'm telling you: I'm out of here."

"You belong with us," he said, gesturing to Allison, who sat in the airport lobby thumbing through a magazine.

"I don't belong anywhere except with my uncle. This clone stuff is too much to deal with. Go to Denver with Allison if you must, but I'm headed home." Then, with a quick sad glance into Chase's eyes, I joined the line departing for California.

The flight was long and lonely, and having a powerful memory proved to be a curse because I remembered every word Chase had said to me. He was in my head and in my heart. I could run away physically, but not mentally.

And when I reached my destination, I stood uncertainly in the airport and stared at the twenty-dollar bill I'd just found in my purse.

Allison! She must have snuck the money into my purse. I wanted to rant at her for interfering and yet thank her for saving my butt. I'd been so determined to return home, I'd never even considered what I'd do when I got there. The two dollars and fifty-three cents in my wallet wouldn't go far. Only Allison had quietly solved this problem.

I was grateful, but I would definitely pay her back. I was not one of her charity projects. I could take care of myself.

Still, the twenty came in handy for cab fare as I instructed the driver to take me to the hospital. I had already called ahead to check on Uncle Jim and was told he was in stable, but critical condition. Crossing my fingers, I prayed that "stable" meant Uncle Jim was well enough to talk.

When I reached the hospital, it was dark, hours after midnight. A new day had started. Sleep was something I'd done in a previous life, when I could close my eyes and feel safe. And although I was exhausted, I would keep moving, not allow myself to slow down.

A slim moon swirled among high clouds and chilly air made me shiver. I hadn't thought to pack a jacket when I'd ran away from Geneva, so it felt good to enter the cozy climate-controlled hospital.

But quick fear hit me when I remembered the last time I'd been here. Geneva and Victor had been waiting — waiting to do horrible tests on me. What if they were here again? The last I'd seen of them had been in San Francisco, but by now they'd had time to fix their car or get a new one and return to Liberty Hills.

Were they here?

My gaze swept the lobby, noting people sleeping in plastic chairs and a few uniformed workers. A custodian swept down a nearby hallway, his gaze focused on dust and dirt, not noticing me. So far, so good.

I moved forward cautiously, staying near the walls, heading for the elevators that would take me to the second floor.

But when I reached out to press the elevator Up button, I heard footsteps behind me. And then someone called, "Varina."

I shrieked and whirled around, terrified I'd find Geneva or Dr. Victor. Instead, I saw a white uniform and friendly smile. "Nurse Burns!" My knees were weak, and I nearly sagged with relief.

"Sorry I startled you," she said, gently patting my hand. "Why, you're trembling. And you look tired."

"I haven't slept much lately."

"No wonder. You poor child, worried about your uncle. How are you holding up, honey?"

"Okay."

"It's past visiting hours, but I'll take you to your uncle. I was heading that way, anyway. His vital signs have improved, but I'm afraid he's still in a coma."

"Oh." Disappointment hit me hard. "I had hoped . . . oh, well . . . Is anyone else there with my uncle? Like Gen— I mean, my aunt Ginny?"

"I haven't seen her."

"Okay," I said with a nod, hiding my relief.

We stopped at my uncle's room, Nurse Burns opening the door for me. "You go on in and talk to him. Maybe he'll hear you and get better quickly."

"You think so?" I asked hopefully.

"Yes, I do." She smiled and gave me an encouraging pat. "Knowing that you're there will help him. I'm sure of it."

"Thanks. Oh, and one more thing."

"Yes?"

I swallowed hard. "Could you stay outside the door and wait for me?"

"My heavens, why?"

"Since the break-in, I've been kind of afraid. Not for any real reason. I'd just feel better if you stayed near."

"I understand. I'm not too busy right now, so I'll sit out here and wait."

"Thanks," I said sincerely. And I was relieved when Nurse Burns didn't ask any further questions.

As the door closed behind me, I faced the still, pale figure attached to tubes and lying motionless on the bed. I noticed some cards and a potted plant on a dresser and realized with surprise that they were from Uncle Jim's faculty friends and students. People out there did care. Maybe everything wasn't so hopeless.

"Uncle Jim?" I called softly, but his eyes remained closed and he didn't respond.

"Please, wake up," I said in a chair by his bed, feeling lost and afraid. "Uncle Jim, bad things are happening and I really need you."

Nothing, except the artificial hum and beeping of machines.

"Oh, Uncle Jim!" I cried softly. "I hate to see you like this. You have to get better. Please try hard. I-I miss you and need you so much. And only you can tell me about my birth . . . the tattoo . . . if I really am a . . ." My sentence trailed off. I couldn't say the "C" word.

I sat beside my uncle for a while longer, talking softly, trying to bring him back to this world. Then the door cracked open and Nurse Burns peaked inside.

"Varina, my shift is over. I have to leave. It's morning and my family will be expecting me to make breakfast."

"Oh . . . that's okay."

"You need to sleep and friends must be worried about you," she pointed out. "I bent the rules by letting you stay this long, but you'll have to leave. I can give you a ride if you'd like."

"A ride?"

"Sure. Even if it's out of the way, I'd be happy to drop you off at your home," she said with a gentle smile.

"A ride would be great!" I replied, then after giving my uncle a soft kiss on his pale cheek, I left the room.

And not long afterward, Nurse Burns stopped her car in front of my home. Uncle Jim's Ford was alone in the driveway and there were no lights on in the house. The house looked deserted, but I couldn't be sure.

I thanked Nurse Burns, then began to walk up the cement entry, hoping and praying that danger wasn't waiting behind the closed front door.

Twenty-Six

I glanced back at Nurse Burns when I reached the front door and gestured that everything was fine. She waved, then drove away.

I only hoped everything really was fine inside my home. But with no lurking white Buick, I felt assured Geneva and Dr. Victor weren't waiting for me. Besides, Geneva enjoyed luxury too much to hang out at my "cozy little" house. She was probably back at her elegant hotel, making more evil plans with Dr. Victor — plans that I hoped no longer included me.

When I reached for the doorknob, my hands trembled, and I fought the urge to flee. Instead, I cautiously stepped inside. No sounds or sense of another presence. So I switched on a lamp and shut the door behind me, locking it securely.

The living room was unnaturally neat and orderly. The cleanup crew Geneva had hired (probably to cover up her own tracks!)

had done a thorough job. The only things out of place were a few dishes in the sink and a coffee cup on a counter. Going into the rooms, I noted that none of the beds, except my own, had even been slept in.

The door to my uncle's office was ajar, and I hesitated before stepping inside and flipping on the overhead light. It was like looking into a museum's staged setting. My uncle's desk, which usually had messy piles of papers scattered like a disaster area, was immaculate. His file cabinet had no half-open drawers with files sloppily poking out. And the books, boxes, bottles, and chemicals on the shelves were arranged with perfection. My uncle's things were in the office, but his personality had been wiped clean. I doubt even his fingerprints remained.

And I hoped nothing important was missing: formulas, notes, journals, addresses . . .

A blinking red light snared my attention and I saw with surprise that the answering machine flashed with messages. Over a dozen unanswered messages!

Curious, I began to play them back. One from my school checking on my absence and a few from associates of Uncle Jim's who expressed sympathy and wished him a speedy recovery. There were also three hang-ups with no messages, and one message from a pesky solicitor (No! We did not want to buy aluminum siding!). Then there was the final message that totally blew me away.

"Hey, Varina. You there? So pick up already. I heard about your uncle. Bummer. Well, anyway, call me back. My number's 555-4494." There was another pause and then the caller added, "Oh, yeah, and in case you don't recognize my voice, this is Starr. Talk to ya later!"

Of course, I recognized the voice with her first "Hey." But I was astonished she'd called me! She'd actually gone to the trouble of finding my number and leaving a message.

Eagerly, I began to punch in her number, but then I glanced at a clock and realized it was only 4:25 in the morning. Oops! People with normal, non-clone lives were asleep at this early hour. My call would have to wait. Besides, I was so sleepy that my eyelids felt so heavy . . .

I yawned. Maybe I'd rest for a while. Yeah . . . that's what I'd do. Then later, I'd call Starr.

When I called Starr, she not only sounded happy to hear from me, but after she found out I was at home alone, she invited me to stay with her.

"Are you sure?" I asked, afraid I'd misunderstood somehow. "But won't your family mind?"

"Only if I let you stay by yourself and didn't ask you over." Starr's laugh was music to my ears. " 'Sides, my grams is visiting her sister and she won't be back for at least a week. You can crash in her room. It's not very big, but it's private and right next to the bathroom — a real plus in our busy house."

"Sounds like heaven." I paused, feeling happy for the first time in days. "This is so great. Thanks. You're a real lifesaver . . . and I truly mean that."

"Let's see if you still feel that way after you meet my younger brother Luther and get a whiff of his stinky socks. We call his room the 'hazardous waste area.' Pee-yew!"

Starr went on about Luther and all his disgusting habits, then switched to her older sister Jazzmine's blind date stories, like the time her date got a popcorn kernel stuck in his nose.

I was laughing so much when I hung up the phone, I had tears in my eyes. It felt wonderful to cry for joy, not heartache, as if I were a new Varina. I liked that idea. I wasn't the same old Varina. This new me was improved, not someone who simply watched others living life, but someone who was out there living it, too. From now on, I would strive to grow stronger, to stand up for myself and not take garbage from anyone.

No one was going to tell me who or what I was ever again. Maybe I had started life as a clone, but how I continued was my choice. And no one could force me to live like a freak if I didn't let them — especially Chase.

TWENTY-SEVEN

The next few days were totally overwhelming.

Starr was pushy, bossy, loud, and impossible — and I loved it! She suggested new hairstyles, insisted I wear a snug Day-Glo purple outfit to school on Monday, and then proudly showed me off to everyone, as if I were her special creation.

I blushed under all the attention, but forced myself to laugh and joke along. I could do this, if I tried hard and didn't worry about what people thought of me. And even guys were thinking about this new improved me. Starr told me in strictest confidence that basketball player Brett had said he might ask me out. He hadn't yet, but I could sense his interest. And going out with a new guy would be the perfect way to stop thinking about Chase.

Wearing Starr's clothes, living in her home, and sharing her life made it easy to forget about danger and science experiments. Yet I could not forget about my uncle.

Fortunately, Starr's mother kindly took me to the hospital every day. She visited a girlfriend who worked in orthopedics while I waited patiently by Uncle Jim's bedside, telling him all about my day, and praying he'd open his eyes or reach out to squeeze my hand.

But nothing.

I hid my disappointment by dressing even more Starr-rageous and making lame jokes with the crowd. I got along fine with everyone: Raylynn, Jill, Janna, Alonzo (Starr's guy), and especially Brett (who called me a "cool babe" and wanted to go out!). The only one who gave me grief was Starr's old best friend Pamela, who glared daggers at me whenever she passed. But I just shrugged off the daggers. Pamela had no power over me.

And then Starr found out about my birthday.

"This Friday? You serious, girlfriend? You gotta celebrate your sweet sixteenth! That's like the eleventh commandment! We have to get busy!"

"But . . . But . . ." I almost blurted the truth, then stopped myself. Sixteen or fifteen? Only Uncle Jim could tell me for sure.

I hadn't meant to mention my birthday,

and immediately tried to change the subject, but there was no deterring Starr. And by the end of school on Wednesday, Starr had planned a huge blowout birthday bash for Friday night. Kids I knew and didn't know would be there. Scary, yet thrilling. And the best part was when Brett came up to me, clearing his throat nervously before he asked me out to my own party.

Nodding, I said yes. *Yes!!!* Then I ran off to tell Starr. Needless to say, she was thrilled.

Swept up in Starr's world, I sailed along and managed to enjoy myself. And when flashes of odd memories started to come, I pushed them aside. Still, sometimes I wondered what was happening with Chase and Allison. Had they found Sandee? Was Eric's family watching out for him? Were they all safe?

For myself, I felt safe at Starr's home. Whenever I went to the hospital, I kept a low profile, often asking Nurse Burns to keep a watch for me. And so far everything was fine. Neither Geneva or Dr. Victor had returned. And I tried to convince myself they never would, that the fear was over.

By Thursday afternoon I needed fresh clothes, among other things, which meant going back to my house. I also needed to check the mail and the answering machine, water the plants and yard, and look for my savings account passbook. Starr's family had been wonderful, but it was time to make plans for myself, seek some independence.

I asked Starr to come with me, only she had a student council meeting. I even considered asking Brett to walk me home so I wouldn't be alone, but decided against it. No way could I tell Brett what I was afraid of and why. Even Starr didn't know the whole story behind my uncle's accident. She thought it was a random attack — and that's what I wanted her to think.

My house looked unchanged, from the solitary car in the driveway to the dishes in the sink that I hadn't bothered to wash. The mailbox was full, mostly with bills, I noticed uneasily. The world of electric bills and house payments didn't stop simply because my uncle wasn't at home.

And new worries hit me. How long could I go off to school and hang out with Starr like everything was fine? The funds in my savings wouldn't go far and I didn't have a job to pay the bills myself. I couldn't even legally drive yet (and probably not for another year if I was only turning fifteen).

If my uncle didn't come out of his coma soon, I could be in real trouble, maybe even forced into the foster care system. Starr's family didn't mind letting me stay while Starr's grandmother was away, but they barely knew me and their home was already crowded. I had no one . . .

Anxiously, I sat on the couch and buried my face in my hands. What should I do? Where could I go? How was I going to get through this?

I don't know how long I sat there, troubled thoughts ping-ponging like wild balls back and forth in my mind. But when I heard the phone ring, I snapped alert.

Automatically, I jumped up and crossed the room, heading for the phone. But sudden fear slammed into me and I froze. Who could be calling? No one knew I was here, except Starr, and she was busy at school. Was it a bill collector, a salesperson, a wrong number? Or worse — what if the caller was Dr. Victor or Geneva?

Another ring. And another. Then the answering machine picked up in the office, my uncle's cheerful voice boomed, "You have reached the Fergus residence. Please leave your name, number, and a short message, and we'll get back to you."

The recorded message was so crisp and clear, like Uncle Jim was in the next room.

"Varina," I heard a different voice come

through the answering machine. "Where are you?"

Chase!!!

"Here! I'm here!" I called, knowing that even with his incredible hearing he wouldn't be able to hear until I picked up the phone.

I stumbled over the coffee table in my haste, then hurriedly picked myself up. I couldn't believe Chase was calling and I couldn't help but be thrilled. I'd missed him so much, and was afraid he hated me after our angry parting. I didn't want him to hate me. I wanted him to like me . . . a lot.

"Guess you aren't there," I heard Chase leaving a message on the machine as I entered the office. "We had some problems in Denver. Too risky to say more. Just be careful. I'll try back lat—"

I reached out, making a wild grab for the receiver. Just as I put the phone to my ear and screamed out "Chase! Wait!" I heard a click.

Too late. He'd hung up.

And when I pressed *69 to try to return the call, all I heard was ringing, over and over.

I'd missed my chance to talk to Chase . . . maybe forever.

Twenty-Eight

By Friday evening I had stopped worrying about Chase and whatever kind of "problems" he'd had because there was a more immediate stress to survive.

My big party — which meant layers of makeup, styled and sprayed hair, borrowed clothes, and a date with Brett. I vowed to just have fun, no worries till tomorrow, when I would make plans. Serious plans — because Starr's grandmother was coming home early on Sunday, which meant I had to leave.

But for now, I was the Sweet Sixteen Birthday Girl! (The fact that I might only be turning fifteen was something I decided to ignore.)

So I sat in a chair while Starr worked her outrageous magic on my appearance — silver dangling earrings, blueberry-scented glitter on my skin, and metallic lavender ribbons woven in my hair. When Starr was through, I was an exotic vision in a flowing multilayered tie-dyed dress. I'd bet even Chase and Allison would be impressed.

Instead of bringing birthday gifts (which would have been too embarrassing from people I barely knew) Starr told her guests to come potluck style and bring something to eat or drink. So the party created itself with Starr's loud sound system blasting music that shook, rattled, and rocked the house.

And there was tall, lanky, surprisingly shy Brett holding out his hand and asking me to dance. This was the first time I'd seen him without a baggy basketball jersey. Instead, he'd dressed carefully in a striped short-sleeved cotton shirt and black jeans, with matching black shoes. I felt flattered, and yet found myself thinking about Chase . . . hoping he was safe.

While I danced with Brett, I moved awkwardly, as if my body responded to a different rhythm. Partygoers whooped and laughed, everyone having a wonderful time in my honor. Yet something jarred, and I knew I was out of sync. I was surrounded by Starr's friends, family, her life. I'd been borrowing her world, instead of creating my own.

Even worse, I was with the wrong boy. An image flared in my mind of Chase clasping my hand snugly in his own, holding me against his chest for comfort, and his brisk yet gentle voice telling me that everything would be okay.

But nothing was okay. And I realized, with regret, I didn't belong here. Maybe I didn't belong anywhere.

Or did I belong with Allison, Eric, Sandee, and Chase?

Clones. Like me.

"This isn't working. I'm sorry." I pulled away from Brett. "I-I can't stay."

"What's the matter?" he asked. "Did I step on your foot too hard? I didn't mean to. Just these giant feet of mine."

"Your feet are great. You're great." *But you're not Chase,* I thought with a sad smile. "I-I don't feel well. I need to sit down. By myself."

I watched disappointment cross his face, and as I concentrated on Brett, I read his emotions. It was like watching a color wheel swirl with changing rainbows. At first he showed a light orange with curiosity, then a blue when he realized I wanted to be alone, and then a silvery flush of something else — longing and desire.

In actuality, all Brett did was shrug and say, "Whatever." Then he turned and went over to slap hands with a basketball player pal.

I hugged myself, trembling a little because it was getting harder to pretend I was a normal girl: assailed by odd flashes of total recall and sometimes reading emotions like vivid neon signs.

Backing out of the rollicking room, I slipped down the hall, toward the rear of the house where a laundry room opened into the backyard. Closing the door behind me, I leaned against a washing machine and shut out the wild party noises. The quiet sounded so good, so relaxing. I could easily stay here until the party ended.

Only I heard a strange sound. A thud and thump. Jerking my head up, I stared through the window to the backyard and saw a face staring back at me.

And I opened my mouth to scream . . .

Twenty-Nine

In a flash of movement and mayhem, the door burst open and the dark menacing man with danger flaring from his bespectacled gaze grabbed me and slapped his strong hand over my mouth. With the other hand, he waved a gun and threatened, "You're coming with me. Now."

No! I wanted to scream, yet I couldn't argue with the black deadly gun.

"Don't bother struggling." Dr. Victor spoke with a rolling Spanish accent. "I won't let you get away like my wife did."

Wife? Could he mean Geneva? They were married?

I had to escape! But no matter how much I squirmed, kicked, and fought to break free, it was no use. Although he wasn't a large man, his hands gripped like steel clamps and he half dragged me out of the room, into the backyard's cold darkness, and away from safety.

He headed for the detached garage, where

I knew with chilling terror he planned to kill me. Dead. Blackness and nothing. Only I couldn't let that happen. I had to save myself — call out for help or fight him off on my own. But how?

Reaching the garage, Dr. Victor yanked open the door then pushed me inside so roughly I stumbled and fell hard on my knees. The pain brought tears to my eyes. Sharp pain that made the fear more real. I huddled on the cold cement ground, hugging myself and staring up at the hand holding the deadly gun.

"Please . . . don't," I whimpered.

"You know who I am, don't you?" His tone was emotionless, holding only curiosity, not the passion of a murderer.

My teeth began to chatter and I hugged myself harder.

"You know more than you should and you've caused me no end of trouble. I remember you well. Even as an infant, you were trouble, 1025G."

A picture flashed in my head of babies with ankle tattoos. And it dawned on me that "G" and "B" meant girl and boy. Chase was 611B, Allison was 330G, and Eric was 229B.

"Don't hurt me," I sobbed. "I-I never did anything to you."

"Ha! Your creation has tormented me for years. The formula was supposed to produce super babies, but not one of you showed exceptional abilities. Failures — especially 611B."

"611B? Chase? But he's not a —" I stopped as memories made my head ache. And again I saw the image of small white-haired Chase screaming "I hate you!" to Dr. Victor.

"Please," I said softly. "Please, just let me go!"

"Not likely!" he snorted. "I'm through with mistakes. You're probably too ignorant to realize it, but you're looking at the most brilliant scientist in the world. I am already quite wealthy and I'm destined for great achievements. Unfortunately, to achieve greatness, past errors must be erased."

I stared at him, disbelieving and more afraid than ever. I clearly saw a violent green-purple aura around him.

The colors of madness.

"I helped create you," he went on, insanity behind his glasses as he held the gun steady. "And it's my duty to terminate that failed project."

"Why now?" I whispered hoarsely, more mind-images swirling in my head. The lab on the yacht, the babies crying, Dr. Victor glaring at Chase.

"I tried to end the clone project thirteen years ago, but my associates behaved unprofessionally."

"My uncle and Dr. Hart."

"Yes," he said with a deep scowl. "I warned them against sentimentality. Experiments are for study, not affection."

"I'm a person, not an experiment."

"You're mistaken," he spoke roughly. "I was there when you were mixed in tubes and created in a laboratory. I analyzed your skin, took blood samples, and even measured your fingers and toes after your birth was achieved."

His clinical words took my breath away and I stared numbly, my heart thumping, my body frozen with fear.

"So where are they?" he suddenly demanded. "Don't play dumb, 1025G. You were in San Francisco with 330G and 611B."

"Six," I muttered, vivid pictures and voices reeling across my brain like a movie. "You called him Six. You were mean to him and he shouted 'I hate you!' You said, 'Enough to kill me?' and you picked up a sharp knife from a counter and handed it to Chase."

"He told you that?" Dr. Victor asked in astonishment.

"No." The images grew stronger and louder. In my mind I heard the long-ago Dr. Victor say to Chase, "Go ahead, try to kill me. Grab the knife. You know you want to!" The doctor ranted more, going on about a failed experiment, but young Chase stood there bravely. He met Dr. Victor's angry gaze with a calm one and said, "Go kill yourself, you creep." Then he ran out of the lab.

"Tell me where the other clones are," Dr. Victor now said harshly. "And I want the Enhance-25X formula, too."

I shook my head, a new picture popping into my head: the lovely woman with auburn hair putting a small bottle labeled Enhance-25X into her pocket. The angel-woman. Dr. Jessica Hart.

"Stop staring like that and answer me!" Dr. Victor shouted. "Or I'll kill you right now."

"Go kill yourself, you creep," I repeated Six's words, trapped between my images and real life. "Chase wouldn't touch the knife. You were angry and threw the knife on the floor. It made a loud noise. Babies cried. I was scared and wanted Dr. Hart . . . but instead, you —" I gasped as I was sucked deeper into the memories. "You-You came over . . . you yelled 'Shut up!'"

"Shut up!" he yelled with a wild fury.

"Then you reached out . . . and . . . and you slapped me!"

"There's no way you can know that! No one else was there!" he cried, the gun trembling in his hand. "Only the babies!"

"Me. I remember."

"But that's impossible!" A crazed look registered on his face, as if he suddenly feared me, and he backed up, bumping into a stack of boxes and losing his balance . . .

He fell backward, his glasses flew off, and his arms flailed up and down, the gun erupting with a large *bang!*

"No!" Dr. Victor shrieked loudly, clutching his leg and collapsing to the ground, blood spreading like a red flood.

Someone was screaming. Me. And I kept on screaming until the door burst open and people rushed inside . . .

THIRTY

Weak. Helpless. I couldn't move, barely had the strength to breathe, and had no desire to open my eyes. Time had passed and I sensed I was somewhere safe. I heard voices around me, felt warm soft blankets, and something poked into my wrist.

Where was I?

My eyes were still closed, and there she was again — the angel lady. Smiling at me, she murmured, "You did good, Varina. I'm proud of you."

"Who are you?"

"Don't you know?"

"Maybe . . . Dr. Hart?"

"Yes, but much more." I heard her words in my head and knew this wasn't just a memory or a dream. I could smell a sweet whiff of lilacs and feel her soft caress of my cheek. A special bond beyond logic connected us. "I love you more than anything," she whispered. "We'll be together . . . someday."

Then I felt a hand touching mine, and I opened my eyes.

"Ah, back to the world of the living!" Nurse Burns spoke cheerfully, leaning over my hospital bed to squeeze my hand.

"Am I okay?" I blinked, looking around and feeling confused. "How did I get here?"

"In an ambulance. Your pulse and heart rate were so faint, we weren't sure you'd make it. Frankly, your symptoms puzzled us. Thank goodness you're better now."

"I guess so."

Then she went on to explain that the police wanted to talk with me. The man who threatened me was also in the hospital under police guard, with a bullet wound to his leg. No one knew what happened and hoped I could tell them.

I nodded, although I could never reveal the whole truth. But at least I could accept the truth about myself. I had been born a clone and I had incredible mental powers of memory and emotions. There was a lot I still didn't understand, but instead of running away, I would face it now.

Time passed in a strange blur. I tried to answer police questions, but I kept falling asleep. My encounter with Dr. Victor had totally zapped me. So I gave into my tiredness and slept.

People came in, like Starr with her mother, yet I was too weary to talk. Starr was concerned for me and I heard her arguing with her mother, insisting I stay with them longer, but her mother refused. Her mother blamed me for bringing violence into their home, and she was right.

I think it was Sunday afternoon when my mind cleared enough to give the police a formal statement and officially press charges against Dr. Victor. I explained that Dr. Victor was crazy. He used to work with my uncle, and for some unknown reason flipped out and became violent.

This seemed to satisfy the police, and they left me alone again. Pampered by Nurse Burns, I felt safe and secure. She told me that my uncle was improving and she predicted he'd come out of his coma soon.

Unfortunately, it wasn't soon enough for me.

Later that day, a man in a business jacket and neat slacks came into my room, announcing he was with child protective services.

"I am not a child," I insisted.

He checked some papers and gave me a steady look. "You are a minor and thus a ward of the county until your uncle recovers."

"I'm almost an adult. I can take care of myself."

"Not according to the law." He shrugged and offered a smile. "Miss Fergus, this isn't a punishment. I'm here to help you out. I'll find a suitable foster family for you to stay with temporarily."

"But I don't want a temporary family!"

"What you want is not my concern. And I'm in charge of your case unless you have an adult relative who can act as your guardian."

"Excuse me —" someone interrupted. "Will I do?"

My mouth dropped open and I stared in astonishment at the commanding blond figure who appeared in the doorway. "Chase!"

"Who are you?" the caseworker asked suspiciously.

"Chase Rinaldi." He stepped forward and held out his hand. "I heard what you were saying, and you don't have to worry about Varina anymore."

"Why not?"

"Because I'm her half brother and I'm over eighteen. I can take care of Varina till Uncle Jim gets better."

Then, with a wicked grin and more creative lies, Chase became my guardian.

Thirty-One

I had so many questions for Chase, but we waited until after I was released from the hospital and on our way back to my house for a serious talk. He told me that Allison was waiting there, too. But he didn't mention Sandee.

Allison was happy to see me and gave me a warm hug. So what if she was rich and gorgeous? She was just too nice to resent. Besides, I had vowed to open up and not shut out friends. So I smiled and hugged her back.

"You poor thing!" Allison cried, ushering me over to the couch and sitting beside me. "I'm so glad the police got that murderer."

"Me, too. Dr. Victor wanted to kill all the clones, like we aren't real people. And he also wanted a formula. Enhance-25X."

"Formula?" Chase raised his dark brows, then pursed his lips thoughtfully. "That makes sense. How else can you explain our powers?"

"And my memory turned out to be a strong power, too," I said. "I freaked Dr. Victor out by knowing things that happened when I was just a baby, and he ended up shooting himself in the leg!"

Chase gave me a startled look, but Allison was totally impressed. For once I was the one surprising her!

"Wow!" Allison squealed. "That's even better than being strong. A perfect memory would be cool! You're so lucky."

"Lucky? Only if the memories are good ones." A dark memory flared and I saw the lab again, Dr. Victor picking up a knife and holding it out to Chase. But Chase turned away and fled the room, which made Dr. Victor so angry he shouted terrible words.

I heard the words clearly this time. And suddenly I knew Chase's terrible secret.

"Varina?" Chase said, coming over and touching my arm gently. "Are you feeling okay?"

"Uh, yeah." I met his gaze; my heart quickened and my fears drowned in his gray-blue gaze. He was my friend and I would stand by him. His secret was safe with me.

"I'm fine," I lied, forcing a shaky smile. "I'm just glad Dr. Victor is in jail."

"Me, too," Allison added with a shudder.

"Of course Geneva is still out there." I gave a weary sigh. "And she scares me even more than Dr. Victor. He's only crazy, but she's totally sane, which is worse."

"Don't worry," Chase said. "We'll watch out for each other."

"Yeah," Allison agreed. "We'll find a safe place to figure out our powers. I'll tell my parents I'm staying with friends, and if they object I'll drop the bombshell about my not being their biological daughter. Then they'll have to listen to me — really listen, for the first time."

"They will." Chase nodded. "And I'll take a quick trip back to Reno, talk to my parents' lawyer and get some money. Then the three of us will work things out."

"Only three?" I took a deep breath. "But what about Sandee Yoon?"

Allison frowned, then tilted her head toward Chase. "You tell her."

"Tell me what? Is Sandee okay?"

"I don't know," Chase admitted. "When we were in Denver, we went to Sandee's home. Her mother answered the door. She'd been drinking, I think. When I asked about Sandee, she just laughed."

"Not a nice laugh, either," Allison added sadly. "And there were little kids in the house with her. The place was a mess and smelled like cigarettes. Poor kids."

"What about Sandee?"

"Gone." Chase snapped his fingers. "She took off over a year ago and no one's heard from her."

"A runaway?" I asked in surprise.

"An older boy yelled out to us that she was following a rock band called Fever Pitch," Allison put in. "But I've never heard of them."

"Me, either," I said, disappointed.

We all were quiet for a moment. Then Allison stood and said she was going to call her parents, leaving Chase and me alone.

I stared across the coffee table at Chase, torn with strong emotions. I still had feelings for him, but knowing his secret frightened me. And when I gazed into his face, that familiar mixture of darkness and light took on new meaning.

"Chase, there's something —" I began, not sure how to finish the sentence.

"You remembered." He frowned. "You know."

It wasn't a question, it was a statement. So I nodded and quickly assured, "But I don't care. Your past doesn't matter. You're a wonderful friend and even more . . . I mean, you're a good person. Dr. Victor had to be lying. There's no way you were cloned from a . . ." My words trailed off.

"Say it, Varina," he said coldly.

"No." I shook my head. "It's not true, anyway."

"Yes, it is." His dark brows narrowed and his jaw tensed. "You can feel the violence in me, and so can I."

I nodded, unable to deny his dreadful secret. No matter how much I resisted, I knew it was the truth; a genetic curse.

Chase had been cloned from a serial killer.